ALWAYS THE SECOND CHOICE

Never the Bride

Book 12

Emily E K Murdoch

Text by Emily E K Murdoch
Cover by Dar Albert

Dragonblade Publishing, Inc. is an imprint of Kathryn Le Veque Novels, Inc.
P.O. Box 7968
La Verne CA 91750
ceo@dragonbladepublishing.com

Produced in the United States of America

First Edition March 2021
Print Edition

The characters and events portrayed in this book are fictitious. Any similarity to real persons, living or dead, is purely coincidental and not intended by the author.

ARE YOU SIGNED UP FOR DRAGONBLADE'S BLOG?

You'll get the latest news and information on exclusive giveaways, exclusive excerpts, coming releases, sales, free books, cover reveals and more.

Check out our complete list of authors, too!

No spam, no junk. That's a promise!

Sign Up Here

www.dragonbladepublishing.com

Dearest Reader;

Thank you for your support of a small press. At Dragonblade Publishing, we strive to bring you the highest quality Historical Romance from the some of the best authors in the business. Without your support, there is no 'us', so we sincerely hope you adore these stories and find some new favorite authors along the way.

Happy Reading!

CEO, Dragonblade Publishing

Additional Dragonblade books by Author Emily E K Murdoch

Never The Bride Series

Always the Bridesmaid (Book 1)
Always the Chaperone (Book 2)
Always the Courtesan (Book 3)
Always the Best Friend (Book 4)
Always the Wallflower (Book 5)
Always the Bluestocking (Book 6)
Always the Rival (Book 7)
Always the Matchmaker (Book 8)
Always the Widow (Book 9)
Always the Rebel (Book 10)
Always the Mistress (Book 11)
Always the Second Choice (Book 12)

The Lyon's Den Connected World

Always the Lyon Tamer

CHAPTER ONE

OLIVIA TOOK IN a slow breath and tried to keep her voice calm. "You cannot be serious, Isabella."

Her twin sister twirled with a mischievous smile. "Why not? 'Tis my wedding, I am the bride, I can surely do whatever I want!"

Her voice was so petulant, so wheedling, Olivia had to sit on the end of her bed and examine her sister before she replied.

She was not serious. For all her peevishness and demanding nature over the last few days, as her wedding to the Duke of Larnwick came closer, surely Isabella was not going to demand *another* delay!

"You have put off this wedding long enough," Olivia said slowly, watching her twin sister pout in the looking glass. "Isabella, be reasonable. The man proposed two years ago!"

"Almost three," said Isabella with a grin. "But he has accepted every other decision to push back the wedding, months and months of it. If I am not entirely happy with the way my hair has been coiffed, I am sure he would understand."

"I am sure he would not," said Olivia, a little more curtly than she had intended.

Well, really. Isabella Lymington was the elder of the twin sisters and had always been one for getting her way, but what girl with thirty thousand pounds wasn't?

This, however, was going too far. Olivia had awoken that morning, hardly believing the day had come. The wedding between Colin

Vaughn, Duke of Larnwick, and Miss Isabella Lymington had been heralded by the *ton* as the most important of the Season...and the next Season...and here they were now, two years after the engagement was announced, and Isabella thought the poor man would accept another postponement?

Isabella moved a delicate curl from one side of her forehead to the other. "No, 'tis completely ruined. I cannot possibly be wed in this state."

Olivia rose from her bed. "Well, let me see if I can—"

"Do not touch my hair!" said Isabella, whirling around with her hands over her hair protectively. "Don't you try, Livvy!"

"Bella, come here," Olivia said calmly, following her elder sister around the room in some sort of wild dance as she tried to keep away from her. "I just need to...it would be easy enough to improve by—"

"Don't you touch me!"

Olivia almost had to laugh. It was so ridiculous as her hands dropped to her sides, and she stopped trying to pin her sister to the wall. Here they were, just weeks after their first and twentieth birthday, and Isabella somehow thought it appropriate to consider her hairstyle more important than all the plans the poor duke had put in place for their nuptials!

The poor man. Olivia's cheeks flamed as she thought of the Duke of Larnwick again. Tall, handsome to a fault, and seemingly besotted with her twin sister.

He had never given her a second glance.

And that was right, Olivia scolded herself silently as she watched Isabella sigh into the looking glass. *Why would your sister's betrothed even notice you?* He had proposed to Isabella within days of meeting the Lymingtons, and he had been patient over the months and years Isabella had made him wait for this wedding.

Your...your fancy that he is handsome is just making you a fool, Olivia told herself. *You need to put him out of your mind. He will be your brother in a few hours!*

"You have an hour," said Olivia quietly, watching her sister. "One hour, and then we will have to depart for the church."

Isabella turned. "Why?"

Olivia almost screamed in exasperation. "For your wedding, Bella!"

"Haven't I already told you, I simply cannot get married in this hairstyle?" Isabella shot back with a serious look. "I will not be a bride if my hair is not perfect!"

Olivia opened her mouth to respond but closed it again. She was getting nowhere with her irascible twin sister. That appeared to be the way between them these last few years. When they had been children, they had been inseparable; more, people had been unable to tell them apart because of their similar looks and natures.

Not any longer. Olivia was reluctant to say it beyond the secrecy of her mind, but…well. Isabella was spoiled now. She was selfish, self-centered, and irritating.

It was this wedding. If the Duke of Larnwick had proposed to *her*, all those years ago…

Olivia blinked. She had become lost in her thoughts, and Isabella was still not dressed. The clock over the mantelpiece showed ten minutes past ten, and they had to be at the church for eleven o'clock – and Isabella was not even in her wedding gown, just a day gown!

"You have put off this wedding for months now," Olivia attempted as her sister sat in the chair by her dressing table. "I think the duke has been very patient, but he is expecting a bride this morning, and that means you!"

"Oh, I do not think Colin would mind," said Isabella lazily, running a hairbrush through her chestnut hair.

Olivia swallowed but had to speak. "I think he would," she said. She remembered the look of exhaustion the duke had given her just days ago at the Braedon wedding. He looked like a man pushed beyond his endurance at Isabella's irritating chatter, and he had not been the only one. *She had been insupportable at that wedding reception.*

"Do you think so?" said Isabella, turning in the chair. "Really?"

"Bella, you accepted his offer of marriage more than two years ago, and the wedding was initially set for just three months after!" Olivia tried to explain in a calm voice, but it was most vexing. "You have agreed on new wedding dates and changed them at the last minute six times now. Do you not think that is odd?"

"No, it cannot be that long," said Isabella airily, placing her sister's hairbrush back on the dressing table and picking up a comb. "No, I think it has been closer to a year."

"When I say more than two years, I say so advisedly," said Olivia bluntly. It was time that spoiled, precious Isabella, the twin who was always right, always beloved, and never spoken to directly, heard a little truth. "It is embarrassing that you cannot remember how long you have been engaged, and it is shameful that you are considering putting off your wedding again! Do you not have any idea how he might be feeling? Have you spoken to him?"

"Oh, Colin doesn't mind me," said Isabella with a grin. "He is besotted with me, Livvy. You must have seen that. He'll do anything I ask, don't you worry. The wedding is postponed."

Olivia swallowed and tried to stay calm, despite intense provocation. It was true, the Duke of Larnwick had accepted all postponements with good grace, but that was his good breeding rather than pleasure at the thought of once again not being wed.

It was embarrassing. Olivia had always been proud to be a Lymington, to come into society and challenge all those stuffy titled people who believed one had to know who one's great-grandfather was to be a gentleman. Their father was in trade. He had made his fortune and raised his daughters to marry well, to act like ladies.

Why couldn't Isabella see that?

"Old Colin won't mind, I am sure, once he realizes how serious this situation is," Isabella was saying. "I mean, look at this curl!"

Olivia sighed and shook her head as she sat back down on her bed. There was no reasoning with her. There hadn't been for the last year, as her twin's antics became more and more petulant. There was no talking to a woman who complained about a hair curl and used it as an excuse to put off her wedding to a duke!

Old Colin won't mind. Really!

Concern seared through her heart. *Colin Vaughn.* He was a man, truly, who had been more than patient, more than understanding. He must be very in love with her twin to put up with her increasingly bad behavior.

The fact that Olivia could not wait to see him at every planned engagement between Isabella and the duke was more than shameful. *It was pathetic!*

It was not wrong to find a man handsome, she knew that. But it had been over two years! She needed to leave her obsession, which was not quite the right word for it, but the way she felt for him was not far off.

She could feel her cheeks flushing. When sister had become engaged to Colin, she should have left those feelings behind. But they had not subsided, and now whenever she was in his presence, she had to be careful where she was looking.

That was easy. She did what most people in Isabella's presence did; look at her.

"I am sure I can fix your hair," said Olivia quietly.

Isabella glanced over at her. "Do...do you think?"

Olivia nodded and moved over to the dressing table. "Come on. This is your wedding we are talking about! Of course we want you to look your best, but as you look pretty, I do not think your duke will mind."

Isabella bit her lip, a hand moving to her hair to tug at her curls.

Was this all nerves, Olivia wondered. A wedding led to the most serious commitment one could make. It was no wonder any woman would be nervous! Spending the rest of one's life with another was hardly a small choice, and once the decision was made, it was difficult to unmake.

"Well, if you think you can," said Isabella, with almost a devil may care attitude.

Olivia smiled through her annoyance. "Excellent. Now, *stay still.*"

"I suppose Colin may not necessarily notice my hair is any different, now I think about it," Isabella chattered away as Olivia attempted to pin her sister's curls, "as I suppose I would not notice whether he changed his hair! But really, 'tis the bride who matters the most in these things, as I was saying to…"

Olivia allowed her twin sister to prattle on. At least it kept her still. Besides, hearing her talk about Colin was…

She was ridiculous. Even hearing about the duke in such a flippant way was painful. How could her sister give so little thought to the man she was about to marry?

Did Isabella love him? Olivia had wondered ever since their engagement had been announced. It had been right after…

Well. The sisters' relationship had never been the same since. Olivia had forgiven Isabella her part in it all, of course, but…well. Once you broke a person's trust, it was difficult to return to how things had always been. And when that person was your identical twin, it was almost impossible.

"There," she said aloud. "Perfect."

Isabella pushed past her sister to get to the looking glass without saying a word. Olivia smiled wryly at her sister's rudeness and wandered to the window seat as her hair creation was carefully examined.

The whole world was teeming outside the window in the street below. London was always busy at the beginning of the Season. Everyone coming from the countryside in desperate need of purchasing the latest fashions for Almack's, card parties, balls, luncheons, and tea parties.

From this distance, three floors up, it was difficult to pick out any individual faces, but there were plenty of groups bustling along: families, sisters, friends, and married couples. Carriages were arriving, depositing people, and then quickly driving away. There they all were, their lives moving forward, changing.

Unlike hers. All she seemed to do was wait for her sister to marry a gentleman she considered the most handsome she had ever met.

There was, however, one thing that caught her eye: a carriage right outside the Lymington London house. It stood unmoving, just...there. It was most odd.

"Look at this," Olivia said, half-forgetting Isabella was supposed to be getting into her wedding gown. "There's a carriage in all the hustle and bustle, just standing stock still. How strange."

"Not really," shot back Isabella quickly. "You have almost got my hair perfect, you know. I don't know why we bother with a lady's maid when you can do it so well. If I wanted flowers in my hair, would you be able to weave them in?"

Olivia's heart sank. She was not a coiffeur creator by nature, just using common sense to pin back the curls created with the papers overnight.

"What kind of flowers?" she said warily. "You know we do not have the time to pick any new ones."

Isabella shrugged as she returned to the dressing table. "Oh, any old thing. Flowers from my room. You know, 'tis funny that in just an hour, I will be the Duchess of Larnwick."

Olivia nodded. She was not jealous of the title. Having a title did not mean much to a Lymington, not when one had a dowry of thirty thousand pounds.

No, it was far more about keeping one's promises. That was what their father had taught them, a core tenant of good business.

"Only make a promise you know you can keep," he always told them.

"Olivia!" her sister said smartly. "I said, I will soon be the Duchess of Larnwick!"

Olivia sighed. *The title, however, seemed to mean a great deal to her sister.* "Yes, you will. It is what you have always wanted, after all."

Isabella smiled and preened a little, twirling the comb in her fingers. "Colin said I was made to be a duchess."

"I am sure he did," said Olivia, not quite managing to keep the sarcasm from her voice. *Well, really.* Of course, he did. He was in love with her! He would say anything she wished to hear.

Though not always. Olivia recalled that very uncomfortable moment at the Braedon wedding, just last week when Isabella was most rude.

"Well, I say," Isabella said. "I have to say that is a crying shame."

"Not here," Olivia hissed.

"What? I may speak as I find, I am sure, and the viscount will think none the less of me for saying that it was a crying shame he gave his bride all the pomp and ceremony she did not deserve," said Isabella with absolutely no care in the world.

And the bride had been very clever and dealt with the situation beautifully, but Isabella had not entirely understood the joke, continuing to prattle on about her wedding plans.

"No one wishes to hear any more about your wedding plans, Isabella!" Olivia had tried to calm her.

"Well, I do not see why not! I will be a duchess, you know, and a duchess..."

Olivia's cheeks seared with heat. It was very like Isabella to ensure that even at someone else's wedding, there was a fuss made over her. That was just the way she was, though now Olivia came to think about it. She hadn't been that way when they had first come out into society when they had been seventeen. She had been...well, they had been more alike. It was only when...

Olivia's lips pursed. *She would not think of that time, she would not allow the pain back into her heart.*

So Isabella was proud she was marrying a duke and wished everyone to know about her great dowry. Olivia did not see the point, but that was Bella.

"Isabella Vaughn, Duchess of Larnwick," Isabella was saying wistfully.

Olivia glanced at the clock. Twenty minutes past ten. "Yes, but you'll also be a wife. Won't that be more important?"

Isabella stared. "Why, what a curious thing to say."

It was always strange looking at one's twin, especially when the two of you were identical. It was like having a mirror constantly at your side, one that twisted and occasionally warped like now, when their hairstyles were so different—a mirror which always showed the best and worst of yourself.

They had shared their entire lives, from the very beginning until now, until today. Today, they would be separated; Olivia would return home with their parents, and the new Duchess of Larnwick would disappear with her husband to his homeland, to Scotland.

It was a strange sort of bittersweet pain. Olivia had not permitted herself to think what her life would be without Bella always by her side. With so many wedding postponements, it hadn't made sense.

Would it be freeing? To no longer be in Isabella's shadow, always compared, always the second choice when it came to cards, or dancing, or conversation? It was all very well being a twin sister, of course, but when one was always compared, never quite enough...

"Oh, a wife, a wife," said Isabella, rolling her eyes. "I do not know why so many people desire it, other than for the chance to run one's household, and that sounds like a lot of work if you ask me."

Flickers of angry flames started to curl around Olivia's heart. To be so flippant, and on her own wedding day!

"You should consider whether the Duke of Larnwick thinks that way," she said curtly, moving to her bed where the beautiful wedding gown, made to her exact specifications, had been laid out. "Now, we need to get you into this gown. Shall I call for Williams?"

Their lady's maid was around here somewhere. If she just rang the bell –

"No, leave it for a moment," said Isabella. She had stepped over to the window and was looking out with a strange expression. Her features softened, and a smile lifted her lips.

And then it was gone, and she was pouting again. "The duke is lucky to have me, you know, Livvy. I am sure he will…he will have nothing to complain about."

"Well, I think he deserves better," said Olivia in an unguarded moment.

Isabella's eyes narrowed.

God in his Heaven, what possessed her to say such a thing! Olivia looked quickly at the wedding gown and tried to collect herself. *This was going to lead to one of their age-old arguments. She just knew it.*

Isabella looked out the window again. "Marriage is supposed to be an adventure, isn't it?"

Olivia hesitated. "Yes."

"But an adventure should be taken with someone you entirely trust, who you love," said Isabella in a strange voice. "Someone you can depend on. It isn't worth taking on the adventure if it is with the wrong person. And what if you don't want that particular adventure? What if you want…something else?"

Olivia placed the gown back on the bed. "Something else? What else is there?"

"Isabella," said Olivia, taking a step toward her sister. "Is…is everything quite well?"

Her sister smiled. "I was just joking, do not mind me. Are my earbobs here?"

Olivia turned to look, utterly lost. "No…no, they must be in your bedchamber."

"I will go and retrieve them."

Isabella was gone before Olivia could say anymore, so she sat in the window seat as she waited. They were going to be late, there was no doubt of that now, but the bride was supposed to be late, wasn't she?

At least this second Lymington wedding could not be as disastrous as the first.

Olivia pushed away the thought. She was not going to think of that. She couldn't. Besides, Isabella was the older sister, and they had grown apart over the years. When the duke of Larnwick had been introduced to them, it had been as 'the Lymington twins'.

Her gaze had drifted back to the carriage standing outside their home, which suddenly jerked forward hurriedly and raced down the street at a great pace.

That had been two years ago, the duke's proposal. Since then, he had grown in her estimations more and more, but that did not matter. It was Isabella whom he had requested in marriage, and that was who would marry him today.

The clock chimed the half-hour, and Olivia looked up hurriedly. So lost in her thoughts, she had entirely forgotten the time.

"Isabella," she called out. "Did you find the earbobs?"

There was no reply.

Olivia sighed. She had undoubtedly caught sight of her hair in a slightly different angle in a looking glass and was even now attempting to perfect it.

"Isabella!"

Her sister did not answer. Olivia swept out of her bedchamber and crossed the corridor into her sister's.

It was empty. Isabella was not there. Frowning, Olivia peered into the adjoining dressing room, but there was no sign of her sister. Two gold earbobs lay on the dressing table, untouched.

They were, however, beside a note written in Isabella's strong hand.

Olivia's heart went cold. No. *This could not be happening, not again.*

She reached for the note and read hastily.

I cannot do it. I cannot go through with this wedding, and if you knew the truth, you would not ask me to. I am more sorry than I can say—when I think of those wonderful times in our favorite place, I know you will all find it in your heart to forgive me. I am gone, and you will not find me. I am sure His Grace, the Duke of Larnwick, will not be too upset.

CHAPTER TWO

"I CANNOT RECALL ever being so upset!" exploded Colin Vaughn, Duke of Larnwick.

Head throbbing, every inch of his body ached with the repressed fury that was coursing through his veins. It was all he could do not to shout again.

He had to control himself. He had to be better than this, but *how could she do this to him?*

"Now, Your Grace, I-I am sure there is a perfectly reasonable," began Mr. Lymington.

"Oh, spare me the theatrics, sir. I do not hold you accountable for this," snapped Colin.

That was true, at least. The last two years had taught him far more than he could ever have expected about his future bride. Most betrothals lasted a few months. Here he was, more than two years after securing the affections—*ha!*—of the woman who today was supposed to become his wife.

Isabella Lymington. Where was she? Where had she gone? And why did she think it appropriate to treat him in such a despicable manner?

Colin tried to calm his breathing. This was getting him nowhere, and with every passing moment, his bride was escaping off into God knows what direction without him. Without any consideration for him at all. *God's teeth that she would act such a way!*

Mrs. Lymington was wringing her hands, muttering about misunderstandings, but Colin paid her no heed. It was clear the family was as shocked as he was, with no conniving here. They had all believed Isabella would marry him that morning, and none was more upset than her mother at her sudden disappearance.

Colin reached the end of the Lymingtons' drawing room and turned to pace back in the opposite direction. The movement calmed him, helped him to think, though there were no great ideas surfacing at the moment.

That she would do this to him! After he had been so understanding, so accommodating of her bizarre decisions to change the wedding date so often. Had he not been caring, loyal, respectful? *And this was the way she repaid him!*

"Never before have I felt like this!" he exploded, unable to keep it within. "To be treated in such a manner, like a common *gentleman*! That wench!"

He was a duke of the realm! To be treated such was abominable, not to be tolerated.

Colin's lungs were on fire as they attempted to draw in sufficient breath for his rage. His heart pounded, a heavy beat he was sure all in the drawing room would hear.

He should have seen this coming. Isabella Lymington had made a fool of him, and his anger was so primal, so instinctual, he was not entirely sure whether he would communicate it coherently.

Isabella Lymington. She was beautiful, wealthy, and relatively well-born. He had not needed her to have a title, just to take his own! How dare she do this to him? *To a Larnwick!*

But no one made a fool of Colin Vaughn. *No one.*

"Does she have any idea what she has done?" he said, the words pouring out before he could stop. "Do you think she comprehends what I will say to her when I catch her?"

"Catch – catch her?" spluttered Mr. Lymington, staring at Colin as though the younger gentleman was mad. "What do you mean, catch her?"

"You cannot mean to go after her, Your Grace," Mrs. Lymington said with some surprise, her hand still at her chest.

Colin stopped his pacing and stared at the two parents. *Well, behind every young woman who had no idea how to behave were a set of parents who had no idea what was due someone of his rank,* he supposed. He shouldn't be surprised. These socially inferior wealthy types came through trade but had little idea how to hold themselves.

Immediately as the thought crossed his mind, Colin censured himself for the injustice of that silent remark. It came from his bitterness, his vanity, nothing else. The poor Lymingtons looked just as confused as to why Isabella had done this as he was.

"I certainly will go after her if I can," he said aloud. "She is my bride, the woman who is to be my wife. You think I would just accept a paltry note like this, with no questions answered, no attempt to restore her to my side?"

Besides, Colin thought to himself, *Isabella Lymington needed to be brought back home, made to marry him, and shown what her place as a woman was. This girl, what did she think she was doing?*

In that moment, his gaze slipped over to the silent occupant of the drawing room. Miss Lymington, the younger twin. It was rather disorientating, looking over and seeing a woman who was the mirror image of his betrothed sitting there quite happily.

But of course, it wasn't Isabella. It was Olivia, the silent and better-behaved twin sister.

Colin smiled wryly. *He had considered Isabella…well, more exciting.* More dramatic, a lady more likely to keep him entertained. There had been little else to choose between them when he first met them two years ago, save that one was the elder.

Miss Lymington noticed his gaze and colored. "Please calm yourself, Mama, Papa. I am sure it will be possible to find Isabella, and…"

"But what would be the point in finding her!" said her father in a despondent tone, dropping into an armchair and allowing his head to fall into his hands. "Oh, that this should happen to us, and after it already—"

"Maurice!"

Colin glanced at Mrs. Lymington, whose cheeks were scarlet. *What was all that about?*

"I mean," said Mr. Lymington hastily, "after the wedding has already been postponed through no fault of your own, Your Grace."

The hackles on the back of Colin's neck rose again. "Yes, this is certainly not the first time your daughter has prevented me from making her my duchess. One would start to think that she doesn't wish to marry me!"

He had said those last few words almost as a joke, something for them to laugh at, to break the tension in the room. What he had not expected was for the sister to flush and the parents to exchange a worried look.

Colin glared at Miss Lymington, and though she flushed, she did not look away.

"Mama, I wish you would calm yourself," she said a little wearily as her mother raised her handkerchief to her eyes once more. "I wish you would not become so hysterical when we have no reason to suppose Isabella is in great danger. All we know is that she is gone."

"Yes, gone!" snapped Colin. "Hastening away, does that not strike you as odd?"

Miss Lymington ignored him. "Mama, the world has hardly come to an end."

"That is easy for you to say!" shot back her mother. "You do not have a daughter missing, out there somewhere in the world with no one to care for her and no one to protect her! Is she warm? Is she safe? Has she eaten today, and how will she eat tomorrow?"

Colin swallowed. *He had not considered that.* She could be in grave danger, and as her betrothed, he was powerless to help her.

Though he could not help but think savagely, she would not be in that position if she had not run away!

"I do not understand it, myself," said Mr. Lymington, raising his head from his hands and looking at his daughter as though she would provide all answers. "I mean, Isabella has been vocal about her excitement for the wedding preparations. Gown, cake, even the flowers in the church had to be perfect. She showed no disinclination for the day before."

"Except," said Miss Lymington dryly, "that this is the sixth wedding date, and once again, we have missed it."

"Yes, yes, good point," said Colin. "Always the date has been pushed back, and always at Isabella's request. Is there a better example of a woman who does not wish to get married?"

There was silence in the Lymington drawing room as his words echoed, and Colin could see they had hit home for Mr. and Mrs. Lymington. Finally, they seemed to realize that though they were certainly not responsible for her actions, *not entirely*, Colin thought they should probably have realized that something was amiss before today.

Colin returned to his pacing. Moving kept him calmer, helped regulate the fury still coursing through his veins.

It was all too embarrassing for words. What was it he had said to Braedon at the ball he had thrown in Isabella's honor not weeks ago?

"And each time it is postponed, it is almost as though the blasted woman does not wish to marry me!"

And what had he said to Braedon when they had gone on a ride?

"It has been arranged for so long, it would be a scandal if either of us canceled."

It was tragic; that's what it was, Colin thought fiercely. *It didn't seem possible that after all of his agonizing, it was Isabella who had decided to leave him!*

Colin's thoughts were interrupted by the loud sniffs emanating from Mrs. Lymington, and he looked at her with a little more compassion now the immediate fury had calmed some. No mother should see her daughter so disgraced, but she was not the only one who had been proven to be a fool by Isabella Lymington's actions.

"...could have done something?" Mr. Lymington was muttering to his daughter, and Colin could see from the other side of the room that Miss Lymington was quietly refuting her father's comments. "You must have known, must have noticed..."

Colin swallowed. This was not what happened to men of fortune and good reputation. Isabella was mocking him, even though she was not here. It was her mere absence that did it.

Christ, this was embarrassing. Girls without titles were not supposed to jilt dukes!

"–should have told us anything you suspected..." Mr. Lymington was saying.

Colin sighed and sat heavily in an armchair on the other side of the room. *God, he could barely stand to stay here, but what other choice did he have?* There was nowhere else he could go in London tonight without causing comment. Even if he went back to his rooms or his club, there would undoubtedly be someone to espy him and report to the scandal sheets that the Duke of Larnwick did not spend his wedding night with his bride in the Lymington house!

He would be the laughingstock of London as soon as this got out, he thought dully. It would not be long. You could never keep anything secret in society, not for more than a day.

"Well, Your Grace, we at least have a few days to decide what to do."

Colin looked up. Mr. Lymington had obviously decided to leave his daughter alone for the present and was now approaching him with a sycophantic smile.

His heart sank. *Christ alive, what now?*

"What to do?" Colin said blankly. "What do you mean, sir?"

"We have informed the guests that the wedding has been...postponed," said Mr. Lymington delicately. "I am sure you will not mind me saying so, Your Grace, but I am afraid it did not take anyone by surprise."

Colin felt blood rush to his head and forced himself to stay seated. The man did not understand that this great insult to the Larnwick name could not go unpunished. *Did they think they could merely put out a story like that and then do nothing?*

"We must go after her," he said. "I will leave in the morning and bring her back to marry me."

Mr. Lymington glanced at his wife for support. "Just a misunderstanding, Your Grace, a simple misunderst–"

"Misunderstanding?" exploded Colin, rising to his feet once again. "Dear God, Mrs. Lymington, Miss Lymington, but your daughter has absconded her family home, her safety, her reputation, all to avoid matrimony to myself! You call that a misunderstanding!"

As he spoke, Colin caught the gaze of Miss Lymington in the corner. She was…not exactly glaring, but the look she was giving him was not a million miles away from disdain.

Disdain? What on earth could she lay at his door in this mess of an engagement?

"Just a simple misunderstanding…" Mr. Lymington was muttering.

Colin rolled his eyes. He had aligned himself with this family, thinking it would be a quick marriage with a generous dowry, and he could disappear back to Scotland where he belonged. Here he was, two years later, stuck in London with an incompetent father and a mother and sister who had apparently not seen a single sign of Isabella's intended escape!

"Misunderstanding?" Colin repeated, pulling out the note his bride had left for him from his waistcoat pocket. "You call this a misunderstanding? 'I cannot go through with this wedding, and if you knew the truth, you would not ask me to'?"

There was silence in the drawing room, though Mr. Lymington did have the good grace to look a little sheepish.

Colin tried to slow down his frustration. "I do not think Miss Isabella Lymington could have been clearer in her intentions, do you?"

Mrs. Lymington sniffed loudly, but Colin's ability to feel sorry for her was wearing thin. There was only one person he felt sorry for in this room, himself.

"I think we can agree that at the moment Miss Isabella wrote this note," said Colin quietly, folding it up again and placing it back in his waistcoat pocket, "she had no desire to marry me, and worse, no thought of my feelings whatsoever!"

Mr. and Mrs. Lymington exchanged a look that was part fear, part embarrassment. They were concerned the duke would eventually make public the scandal, even if it were to explain why he was returning to Scotland with no bride.

Colin was half-tempted to do it. *This could still be salvaged if she could be found.*

Miss Isabella Lymington clearly had a mind of her own, and it did not appear any family responsibilities or promises made meant anything to her whatsoever.

Christ, it was such a mess.

"Where did she go?" he said gruffly. His gaze moved from father to mother. "Do you know?"

Mrs. Lymington, the perfect picture of distraught motherhood, said, "She could be anywhere, Your Grace. For all we know, she was forced to write that letter at knifepoint! A man could have come into the house and made off with her!"

Her voice faded away as she succumbed to silent sobs, face hidden by her handkerchief. Mr. Lymington rose and gripped his wife's shoulder, his face pale.

To believe your daughter, your very flesh and blood to be out there in the world, without any knowledge of her safety…

He only had to worry about his reputation.

"We cannot hope to keep this quiet forever," he said. Mrs. Lymington squeaked, but Colin was relentless. "This will get out, especially when I am seen out in public without her."

"You could always just go back to Scotland."

The words were not spoken with malice, but there was no warmth in them either. They had been uttered by her twin. Miss Olivia Lymington met his gaze fiercely.

Colin almost laughed. He had almost forgotten she was there, the little minx, and now she had the audacity to spring that opinion on him? *Had she no idea how her chances for a good match were now damaged?*

"Why do you say that?" he asked.

"Well," Miss Lymington said, as though carefully weighing her words. "You speak much of your love for your country, Your Grace. You spend a great deal of time there, and on the few occasions that you make the journey south, you speak more about your desire to return than your enjoyment here."

Colin's mouth almost fell open. *She was an observant minx.* Far more than her sister. He could not remember a single instance where Isabella asked about his homeland. He did speak of Scotland a lot, now he came to think about it, which was no great surprise. That was where he had been born, where his lands were.

What was odd was how entirely the wrong twin had noticed.

"I just thought, with Isabella now gone," continued Miss Lymington in a conversational tone, "that you would just go back. You never took Isabella there, so there will be no comment. You can simply say the engagement was broken off."

It was such a sensible course of action that Colin was a little concerned he had not thought of himself.

But Colin knew he would never simply return to Scotland empty-handed. His pride would not permit it.

"Olivia Lymington, how dare you suggest such a thing!" Mr. Lymington's outrage cut through Colin's thoughts. "You know Isabella must be brought back and made to marry him!"

"Just…just go back to Scotland without Isabella?" Mrs. Lymington was looking at her daughter as though she had never met her before.

"What did you know about Isabella's plans for this, Olivia? Tell me the truth, girl, did you know she was planning to leave?"

"Of course not!" Miss Lymington protested, but only then did her gaze drop to her hands. "I had no idea she was intending to leave like this, except…well, I knew she was not taking the whole thing seriously."

Colin took a step toward her. "Seriously?"

Miss Lymington did not respond as her father chastised her. "Answer His Grace, girl!"

"I cannot have been the only one to notice," she said quietly, obviously discomforted by the attention but continuing on under the watchful glare of her father. "She…well, has been far more interested in the wedding than the marriage. The dress, the diamonds, all those things. It's the wrong way round, isn't it?"

She looked between her parents, then Colin.

Colin was impressed, despite himself. *An observant one, indeed.* It appeared her parents were less than impressed.

"You should have told us you harbored suspicions Isabella might not go through with the match!" hissed Mrs. Lymington. "You should have said she intended to run away!"

"I had no comprehension that was the direction of her thoughts," protested Miss Lymington, "and I had no idea she had followed through on that thought until I read the note."

Colin pulled it from his waistcoat pocket again.

Fury rose in his heart. After the months of negotiations, decisions, compromises, pushing back the date again and again, he had believed today to be the end of this nonsense.

But no. It was the day she most embarrassed him.

"'Tis a scandalous thing indeed," said Mr. Lymington heavily, "but do not fear, Your Grace. We can ensure you a Lymington bride."

Colin frowned. "Now what do you mean by that?"

"Well, isn't that the obvious solution?"

Colin looked where the older man was pointing. 'That' appeared to be his daughter, whose cheeks turned scarlet.

"Her sister, an exact match," said Mr. Lymington triumphantly. "Why not marry her?"

Chapter Three

OLIVIA FELT HER cheeks flush, but there was nothing she could do. The words had been said by her fool of a father who evidently had no idea the pain he was causing his second daughter, and now the entire room was staring at her.

And it was not her mother's gaze that mortified her. It was the Duke of Larnwick, looking at her as though he had only just remembered she was there.

This was utterly insupportable! She needed to speak, needed to refute such a foolish suggestion as soon as possible.

But she couldn't. Her mouth was dry, throat closing up as her father's words rang in her ears.

"Her sister, an exact match. Why not marry her?"

After everything she had done to try to keep this marriage on track! After she had spoken over Isabella's foolish words, hidden her sister's boredom around the wedding planning, tried as best she could to keep the duke happy!

It was her lot, Olivia supposed silently, that she would be forced to encourage her sister, who did not seem to understand how fortunate she was to marry a man that she herself had wanted...*well, not exactly wanted...she liked him!*

And now she was to be offered up as some sort of consolation prize?

"What did you say?" The duke's face was impassive, and even as Olivia's eyes snapped over to him, he did not look at her.

No, his attention was focused on her father, who evidently believed he had offered an ingenious way out of their predicament.

"I said," repeated her father with a smile, "why not take Olivia? I mean to say, she looks precisely the same after all. All girls do, up to a point, but this is particularly unique. Isabella's identical twin, you see?"

Second choice again, thought Olivia dully as the heat of embarrassment started to fade. *Well, it was not as though she was unaccustomed to it, but to have it so blandly spoken, and to His Grace, too!*

Sometimes she wondered whether her parents were trying to infuriate her.

The Duke of Larnwick stared, and Olivia felt that dratted flush return. *If only she could hold her nerve!* The curiosity in his face was something she should welcome. After being utterly ignored whenever Isabella was in the room, any attention was in some way gratifying.

Olivia swallowed. *But not like this.* If any man, let alone the duke she had taken such a fancy to, was going to look at her as a potential bride, it should be on her merit.

Not because the better option had sailed out of their lives without as much as a backward glance.

She had to tell them she could not be served up as a second course because the first was not quite to someone's taste!

"I..." she tried. Words utterly failed her. *Had there ever been a moment in her life more mortifying than this?*

Yes, there was, a little uncomfortable voice reminded her. *Just one. And that was Isabella's fault, too.*

"You suggest to merely swap the one for the other?" said the duke slowly.

Olivia's stomach twisted painfully. *If only she had never noticed him.* If only she had considered him with indifference, had seen him purely as her sister's admirer and no more.

But no, she had to notice that the Duke of Larnwick was not only handsome but kind, caring. He had a free spirit that did not blossom here in London, but Olivia was sure she understood it. *Understood him.*

He had been precisely the sort of gentleman she had hoped her parents would choose for her…but they had chosen Isabella.

She was not going to be parceled off whenever her parents thought she 'would do'.

"Well, what a wonderful idea!" her mother exclaimed, tears quite forgotten and handkerchief dropping to her lap. "You are quite the clever man, my dear. Yes, take Olivia."

"No."

Olivia had not spoken loudly. She had not needed to. That one syllable had echoed in the room and caused everyone to look.

Her gaze met the duke's, and she fought the instinct, ever-present in his company, to look away. This was not a situation a young lady had probably ever found herself in, but Olivia was sure, nonetheless, that there was only one outcome.

She could not marry the duke merely because she looked like her sister! Worse, she could not marry a man she had found herself drawn to because he was available after her sister had *gone missing!*

It was not as though she had done anything untoward to gain his attention. Quite the opposite; Olivia had become accustomed to fading into the background when Isabella was there.

The duke was her sister's betrothed!

Did her parents think she could forget the last two years?

The duke had resumed his pacing, an endearing habit she had noticed about a year ago when Isabella had asked to postpone the wedding the day before they were due in church.

A small smile crept over her face. She had quickly realized that Larnwick only paced when under extreme pressure and did not know what to do with himself. She knew him better than Isabella did, had watched him more closely. Her sister was interested in being the center of attention from the whole room. *One gentleman was never enough.*

Olivia swallowed down her bitterness and tried to concentrate. The suggestion had been made and could not be unmade. *The question was, what did His Grace think about it?*

She caught his eye for a fraction of a second before he resumed pacing. It was enough.

Well, stranger matches have been made before, that little voice reminded her. It was foolishness, it was wild, it was...

A possibility, Olivia admitted to herself. Was this the way she finally got her happily ever after? The Duke of Larnwick was a good man, and that was enough in the world of matchmaking.

If only she thought her parents were indeed in earnest.

Her thoughts had taken such a detour of her emotions, Olivia was surprised to find only a minute or so had passed. Her parents were still looking at her expectantly, as though it was her turn to say something.

Olivia moved her hands to her lap. What did he think? *The Duke?* Was he considering this, too? Could he see merit in it? *Would he ever be able to look at her and not see Isabella?*

"You must think me a fool, sir!" burst the Duke at her father. There was scorn in his tone. "Are they so interchangeable? I don't want the second choice. I want Isabella!"

If only the ground would swallow her up. Olivia closed her eyes in horror.

Second choice. It was degrading to hear that word on his lips.

This was Isabella's fault. Isabella and her father. Neither understood what it was like to be always the second, always bringing up the rear, always behind, never in front. The younger twin, the second daughter, the one everyone invited but could never name.

What had she done to deserve such censorship? What ignominy would she endure! To be offered out like an unwanted parcel, only to be rejected by the recipient!

"Oh, I do not know about that," said her mother hastily. Olivia knew not to expect praise and was proved right when Mrs. Lymington continued, "After all, one can barely tell them apart! You are getting the best of Isabella when you look at Olivia, surely!"

"I cannot tell them apart most of the time," said her father cheerfully. "I often think they are the same person!"

Olivia tried to remain calm, but the temptation to shout was growing. Surely this was not what her life was supposed to be? Merely considered an extension of Isabella, a reflection of her, a very good one as though that was somehow merit in itself?

No, this was intolerable. Her parents continued to chatter on about how similar they were, how twins were always so similar, did he not know?

Olivia could not speak. She was too busy attempting to keep her temper. The last thing she needed was to embarrass herself further by speaking sharply to her parents before the duke!

"I do not think you understand," he was saying to an increasingly passionate Mrs. Lymington, who appeared determined to get at least one daughter married off today. "I proposed to Isabella, and it is she I wish to marry."

"...almost thought Isabella was Olivia this morning, so similar," her father was saying.

Her mother was trying to speak to both of them and succeeding very poorly at both. "No, that *was* Isabella. I do not see the difference, Your Grace."

"Enough."

The room fell silent, and all eyes once more turned to Olivia, but this time she was ready. She had calmed her temper, for the most part, and she had a plan.

"I quite agree enough," said the duke shortly. "You are not Isabella, Miss Olivia, though I am sure you are very...very nice."

Olivia almost rolled her eyes. *What praise.* "Indeed. What I suggest is that instead of attempting to find an alternative to Isabella, we go and find her. The real thing, as it were."

It was not entirely possible to keep the sarcasm from her voice, but Olivia thought, given the circumstances, she did rather well.

Mr. Lymington blinked. "What do you mean, the real thing?"

"Go and find her?" repeated her mother.

Olivia nodded. "Go and find her. Then His Grace will have the bride he wants."

Once again, she had tried to keep her voice entirely neutral. Was it not bad enough she had been passed over before? No, she had to be passed over again, and this time explicitly.

The sooner they could find Isabella and make her marry the duke, the better. Then Olivia would finally be able to leave thoughts of His Grace behind.

"B-But what–what on earth do you mean?" spluttered her mother. Olivia did not look at her. She was too busy looking at the duke, who had halted his pacing and was examining her most curiously. "Go and find her? My dear Olivia, you appear to have forgotten that we have no idea where she is, nor who she has gone with!"

"You think I have not considered going after her myself?" her father said in a condescending tone. "Where to start, that is the problem, of course. Where to start?"

Olivia hesitated. The suggestion had come from deep within her. An instinct, if she could put it that way. She may look like Isabella, but she certainly did not think like her.

Besides, a very contrary part of her did not wish to help Isabella. It was not as though her sister had ever shown much interest in the Duke of Larnwick. No, her twin was far more enamored with money, wealth, prestige, and titles.

Perhaps she had found someone better. But who was more impressive than a duke?

And this was not all about her, was it? That was the trouble with society, and the *ton*, and all its rules and restrictions. If Isabella was not found and made to marry the man, what would become of her, them all?

No gentleman would wish to form an alliance with a Lymington girl, not after the eldest postponed her wedding several times, then disappeared on the day of the wedding.

Olivia sighed. She could worry about Isabella all she wanted, but she had to think of herself, too. Unless they found Isabella, and soon, the family name would be ruined. They had to do something. They could not just sit here and act as though Isabella was, at any moment, to realize her mistake and walk right back into their lives.

"If we can just find her, I am sure she is regretting her choice of action already," she said quietly, more for the duke's benefit than anyone else's. "I am sure if we could catch up with her, explain things to her, the duke could tell her his feelings..."

Her voice faded away as Olivia's gaze met his. It was a rather presumptuous thing to suggest that he bare his heart to her sister.

Did the Duke of Larnwick have feelings for her sister, deep, passionate feelings? Or, as it appeared to her, was he merely piqued that she had dishonored him by running away?

As she thought back to the things he had spoken of since Isabella's escape, anger, embarrassment, shame on his name, fear of the gossips finding out, scandal sheets...

Nothing about love. Nothing about a broken heart.

Olivia was no child. She knew most matches were made for convenience, family advancement, money, or a mixture of the three.

That was why Isabella's engagement with the duke had been so surprising in the first place. The Lymingtons had money, true, but no great title, no connections, nothing that would make them a likely proposition for a duke.

She had always assumed it was because Larnwick had fallen in love.

"That would be all very well if we knew where she was," snapped the duke. "If her location was known, I would go there myself, but she could be anywhere!"

Something nudged Olivia's memory, and she smiled. "Please, may I have the note?"

"Why?" The duke appeared to realize he had been rude and added, "if you please."

Olivia merely raised an eyebrow. *He was not father nor brother that he could make demands of her.* "Please, Your Grace."

For a moment, she thought he was going to refuse it, but after a moment's indecision, he thrust a hand in his pocket and proffered the letter with a very bad temper.

"I do not know why you want it," he said bitterly, returning to his pacing. "There is not a single mention in there of where she has gone."

"That," Olivia said sweetly, "is because you do not know my sister."

She had probably offended him now, but she did not see his expression because she was too busy examining the letter.

...when I think of those wonderful times in our favorite place.

She smiled. Even Isabella could not help herself.

"Listen to this," she said, and she saw the duke cease his pacing. "When I think of those wonderful times in our favorite place. See?"

There was nothing but blank faces from both her parents and the duke.

Olivia sighed. "Brighton. She has gone to Brighton."

Larnwick hastened forward and snatched the letter out of her hands. "Are you sure? How can you be sure? There is no mention of Brighton in this note."

It was all she could do not to allow the frustration into her voice as she replied, "I thought everyone had decided that we are essentially the same person?"

The duke had not stepped away, and Olivia was forced to look upward from her seat into his dark and fiery eyes.

"You know," he said quietly, "perhaps you are. In many ways, I cannot tell you apart. Are you willing to come with me to help track her down? You know her old haunts?"

Olivia swallowed. "*Our* old haunts, yes."

What was she thinking? She could not go gallivanting off with a duke!

But his comment was ringing in her ears.

"In many ways, I cannot tell you apart."

How was that possible? Over the last two years, he had spent hours with Isabella, offered her his hand, seemed genuinely frustrated whenever she postponed their nuptials, and yet he could not tell her apart from his bride?

"I will go with you," said her father, standing slowly. "Going after her is the right thing, and if Olivia knows where she has gone…"

"Oh, but who will stay here with me?" Olivia's mother looked genuinely concerned. "Who will protect me, who will keep the gossip out of society's grip?"

Mr. Lymington hesitated, and Olivia bit her lip. Her father was needed here.

"You never know," she added quietly, "Isabella may return here. She may regret her choice when she realizes the consequences of her actions."

She caught the duke's gaze, and for a moment, there was a flash of understanding. *Isabella was not coming back. Not of her own accord, anyway.*

"Yes, I agree with Mrs. Lymington," said the duke gruffly. "You must stay here, sir, to protect your remaining family. I am sure Miss Olivia and I will only be gone a day or two. We will be back before you know it!"

"But…but…" Mr. Lymington did not entirely know how to proceed, but as he glanced between Olivia and the duke, it was clear that he was concerned.

Olivia gritted her teeth. If she could not go with the duke, then he would never find her. But her father's apparent concerns were valid. She should not be traveling with a man, unmarried as she was, with no chaperone!

"It will be quicker with two," said the duke. "Quicker to travel, and quicker to come back. Besides, it may be a fruitless journey. Perhaps she has not left London yet for Brighton and may still come to her senses."

Olivia caught her father's eye and tried to smile. They both knew Isabella far better than that. Isabella may struggle to make up her mind, but when she did, she stuck to it. There was a high possibility that even if she and the duke were able to catch up with Isabella, he might not get what he wanted from her.

Still, they had to go.

"And you can leave first thing tomorrow?" her father asked.

"Yes, absolutely," the duke said. "Otherwise, the trail could go cold."

Only then did the truth of what she had agreed to sink in, and Olivia felt her cheeks pink again. *She was going on a journey with the Duke of Larnwick, just the two of them!* It was the last thing she could have expected after today.

How on earth would she manage to keep her feelings to herself?

And what would they do when they finally caught up with Isabella?

Chapter Four

THERE WAS NO amount of rubbing his eyes that could entirely wake the Duke of Larnwick. Not after the night he had just had.

He had barely spent more than a few hours in bed, worse luck, and even when he managed to clamber in and close his eyes, his mind did not stop.

As he slumped into his carriage and leaned back, his eyes closed. *What a night.* What a day! He was already exhausted, and it was barely eight o'clock in the morning. He had the entirety of today to suffer through, hardly made easier by the company he would be keeping.

Colin opened his eyes. *God, he was a fool.* Why had he not seen any of this coming? For all his impressive words to Braedon about not wishing to get married and just going along with it because the engagement had gone on for too long—*all true*—it was still not the total of his thoughts about his intended marriage to Miss Isabella Lymington.

She was beautiful, rich, and quite publicly engaged to him.

Yet he should have seen this coming if he had been any sort of gentleman with any sort of brain. Had he not been given, time and time again, sufficient evidence to believe Isabella had no desire to wed him?

The sheer number of times she had postponed the wedding?

"Y'Grace?"

Colin jumped. So lost in his thoughts, he had not realized his driver had been standing by the door. For how long, he was not sure.

"Yes, Smith?" he said, a little more testily than he would have liked.

The driver, however, knew the vagaries of the Scotsman's temper and merely smiled. "Are y'ready, Y'Grace? Off to the Lymingtons' house, are we?"

Colin nodded. His voice was hoarse after so much talking the night before, though he would undoubtedly sit in silence with the twin.

"Right y'are, Y'Grace," said Smith happily.

The door to the carriage was slammed shut, rocking the coach again as Smith mounted, and with a flick of his whip, they were away.

It was a gentle carriage ride. They had to go across London to pick up whatshername Lymington, for a start, giving Colin ample time to consider just how he had managed to get into this confounded position.

Isabella Lymington. He could picture her perfectly in his mind, not that he would need to, once the twin had stepped inside. *Uncanny, their similarity was.*

But then, Miss Isabella's appearance had not much changed in the two years Colin had known her. By God, he had been obsessed with her then. Taken by her beauty, her charm, that witty way she always had a response to anything…

He had been unable to keep away. The engagement had been announced within weeks.

Colin shook his head. He had been so pleased with himself then, so proud he had managed to snare one of the most beautiful women to enter society.

Only after a year could he see his obsession had blinded him. The attraction was entirely one-sided, and it had taken him another few months to realize his desire had faded.

They were bound to each other by honor, and that was all. At the moment, that did not feel like very much. Colin had known it. He had spoken the truth to Braedon. He had sought a way out of this engagement, at least in the privacy of his own heart, and now he was paying the price for that inconsistency. Now the very woman who had been promised to him had disappeared, and it was his damn fault for even thinking of it.

It was a strange sort of divine punishment, but then that was often the way of it.

Colin glanced out of the window. Though the sun was starting to come up in the early wintery way it did, there were few people on the streets. Most of London would have been gallivanting out last night to parties, balls, and card parties.

Wedding receptions.

Colin swallowed. If anyone knew Miss Isabella Lymington would rather run out of her parents' home, unaccompanied and unprotected, than marry him…

Everyone would assume he was an ass! Or worse, a blaggard!

Perhaps, he thought dully as his carriage turned a corner, *he should have just broken with her weeks ago after that disgraceful behavior at the Larnwick ball.* It had been his party, so to speak, hosted in her honor.

The very least she could have done was speak to him.

He should have known then. He should have known as soon as he caught sight of Isabella across the ballroom, and his heart had sunk rather than sang.

And so despite fate, or chance, or whatever it was handing him the opportunity to break with her…he was going after her.

It would not have made sense to anyone else, and Colin knew that. But he was a duke, and far more importantly, a Larnwick. No one slighted a Larnwick like this. It was intolerable and not to be borne.

He would return to Scotland with a Lymington bride, or not at all.

And by God, he missed his homeland. It still amazed many of his acquaintance in London when he mentioned he had no desire to be in town. They marveled at his lack of interest in the opera and laughed at his inability to navigate the crowded, smelly, dirty streets, which all looked the same to him.

There was little in London to recommend it, as far as Colin could see. True, there were a few parks that were pretty enough, he supposed. But how could one even start to go about comparing Hyde Park with the Highlands?

Scotland. The place he was born, the place he belonged. Sometimes he wished to be back there so much, his heart physically ached, and he had to instruct his butler to bring him one of his finest whiskies which he would drink slowly, savoring the taste of home.

Colin looked out of the window with a start and saw they were on the Lymingtons' street. The carriage slowed and stopped right outside their abode, but Colin did not get out. He was not in the mood for civilities, not after last night.

It was not the Lymingtons' fault Isabella had disappeared. The parents seemed utterly lost, and the sister…

Colin swallowed as the carriage rocked, his driver placing some luggage on the top rack.

"Here y'go, Miss," said his driver cheerily as he opened the door and awkwardly helped Miss Olivia Lymington into the carriage.

"Thank you," she murmured, taking a seat opposite Colin yet avoiding his gaze, a reticule clasped in her hands and a traveling cloak around her shoulders.

Colin could not help but stare. *It was the most strange thing.* He knew his intended bride intellectually, Isabella, was miles away. Hopefully in Brighton, as that was where they were headed.

And yet, her exact double was seated before him. *Double save for the fact that she had not immediately started talking about herself,* he thought wryly.

"Good morning," Miss Olivia said quietly.

Colin did not speak but inclined his head. His silence appeared to have a confusing effect on the twin, her cheeks flushing and her gaze shifting to the window.

He looked out, too. There stood Mr. and Mrs. Lymington on the doorstep, both looking very tired and Mrs. Lymington with that perennial handkerchief in her hand.

"Be good," she called out in a loud whisper, as though worried the neighbors may deduce what was occurring. "Find her quickly. Do not eat anything that you do not know—"

"Send the bills to me," interrupted Mr. Lymington with a concerned look at Olivia. "Wrap up warm. Speak to no one but His Grace, and at all times…"

"Tell Isabella we are not angry with her," said Mrs. Lymington, the words spilling out of her mouth as though unable to help herself, though she glanced with a worried expression at her husband. "And advise her to—"

Colin had had enough. He needed no more platitudes for the woman who was supposed to be his wife. He rapped on the roof of the carriage, and it lurched forward almost immediately as Isabella, no, *Olivia* waved goodbye to her parents.

She was the twin, damnit, he reminded himself. It was undoubtedly going to be rather disorientating to have her on this journey, a woman who was the mirror image of the female he had fallen into, then arguably out of love with.

Still. She would be useful, that was certain. It had been she who had understood the hint of Brighton in the note still in his waistcoat pocket.

Though her gaze had not settled on him, preferring to examine her lap, Colin looked at her unashamedly. Well, she was his guest, after all. *Why not look at her?*

His breath was almost taken away by the similarity with her sister. She was so like Isabella; the same chestnut hair, the same full lips, inquisitive eyes, the gentle slope of her neck forming her slight build.

If he had been told the woman before him was Isabella, he would have believed them. There was nothing to tell them apart, nothing.

Well, hopefully, she would be quiet on the journey and not disturb him. They would not have to worry about conversation, the rules of society not applying in this rather unusual circumstance.

Still, he had to be polite. His breeding ached to make small talk, and if he did so now, in the first five minutes of the journey, he could return to blessed silence for the rest of the trip.

"I...I hope you are well, Miss Olivia," Colin staid stiffly.

She caught his eye and then returned her gaze to her lap. "Yes, Your Grace, I am perfectly well. A little tired after yesterday."

Colin nodded. *Yesterday*. Yesterday, he should have been married. Yesterday his bride should have met him at the altar, but instead, he was stuck with her twin as they attempted to find the first.

It was all such a mess, hearts and reputations all ruined if they were not careful. But if they could find her, before any news of such a calamity got out, no one would ever have to know.

What a blessed relief that would be. What did it matter if Isabella had last-minute jitters if all would be well in the end?

Yes, that was what they would do, Colin decided. They would find her in Brighton, he would wed her there, and return to London as man and wife. Mr. and Mrs. Lymington would undoubtedly be sad to miss the nuptials themselves, but they would be far more relieved that their daughter had been found, and more importantly, *married*.

Colin shifted uncomfortably in his seat as the carriage rattled down the London streets. It was most strange. Just the mere thought of Isabella was making his body respond, as it so often did, but now he was in a carriage with an exact replica of the woman.

Olivia. She was not helping to get his body under control. He supposed it was natural, given that they were identical.

They were starting to leave London, the buildings now smaller, more spaced apart.

And then she spoke into the silence. "I had always hoped to go back to Brighton. But not like this."

Colin's heart sank.

What was she thinking?

His gaze flickered over her. In any other situation, he would have grunted rudely, but this was Olivia Lymington. He had courted her twin for two years now, and there was not that much difference between them. All he had to do was treat her like Isabella. It was not as though the twins were that intellectual. *The effort required would be minimal.*

"Yes, I am sure," he said with a swift smile. "You must miss seeing the regiments who winter there over the season, and the balls, and card parties, and such things."

His duty to make light conversation over, Colin looked out of the other window. *They could not get to Brighton quick enough.*

But the silence was unexpectedly broken.

"No, actually," said Miss Olivia quietly.

Colin's gaze moved, despite himself, over to the twin. "No? What do you mean, no?"

"Precisely what I say," said the twin demurely. "No."

"But Isabella loves wintering there, she told me herself. She likes to see all the flags over the tents, fluttering in the breeze as they—"

"Well, I like Brighton in the summer," interrupted Miss Olivia in a most disobliging way. "I like the heat. Walking along the beach, feeling the sand between my toes. Taking a bath, if I am fortunate and my father permits it. Summer was always my favorite time to go."

It was rather a long speech. Colin sat in amazement. It was such a strange response for Isabella, but of course, this was not Isabella. She may look like her, sound like her, but there were obvious differences between the sisters he had not, until now, been party to.

So. One liked winter and all the showy decoration and flattery she received, and the other enjoyed summer and the solitude of a bath. *How strange*. Perhaps there were some small differences after all.

"I never was one for beaches," he found himself saying. "I like mountains."

"I have never seen a mountain," said Miss Olivia, still looking out the window.

Colin's jaw dropped. "Never seen a mountain!"

It was incomprehensible. *How could one live without seeing the splendor, the majesty of a peak that looked over God's creation?*

"No," she said.

"Oh, Miss Lymington, you absolutely must! The climb up, taking everything from you, forcing you to confront your humanity, your frailty, and the view from the top! The air, cleaner than anything you have ever experienced. Knowing you are but one step from God, viewing his creation as he does."

Colin's voice faded away, embarrassment catching up with him. He had never spoken like this with Isabella, for she had never shown any interest in his homeland, even after copious invitations.

"It sounds wonderful," said Miss Olivia, eyes bright, and then remembering herself, her shoulders slumped, and she looked down. "I suppose I shall never see such things, but I am sure you are eager to get back there."

"Yes. Yes, with my bride," said Colin shortly.

The mention of Isabella, though not by name, was sufficient to end the conversation. Silence fell for several minutes as Colin attempted to empty his mind of all thought.

It was impossible. Not with Olivia seated opposite.

Thankfully, she seemed as undesirous of conversation as he was. Colin refused to allow himself to look at her. For about ten minutes. After that, there was nothing else for him to do, the view from the carriage window now naught but blurred fields and hedgerows.

Was she *doing embroidery?* Colin blinked, but the item between her hands did not change. *Yes, embroidery, careful tiny red stitches slowly becoming roses.*

It was remarkably fine, and he could not help but say, "Pretty."

"Thank you," she said quietly.

Her tone did not invite further discussion, but Colin was bored. He should have thought of this, brought a book or something. If he was not so afraid he would start to snore, he would take a nap, get some much-desired sleep.

But instead, he found himself saying, "You know, you are good at that. Surprising."

Miss Olivia's eyes met his. "What do you mean?"

"Well, Isabella hates embroidery, doesn't she?" Colin said easily. "Not only that, but she is awful at it. I know, she has shown me some of her work, well, if you could call it work. I was polite, of course, but it was nothing compared to yours."

It was quite a pretty compliment, Colin thought, and he had expected a blush, a smile, a thank you for his compliment.

Instead, she frowned. "Your Grace, I admit I feel a little strange pointing this out to an educated man like yourself, but you…you do realize that we are different people? Isabella and I…we might be twins, but that does not make us identical through and through. We just look alike."

Colin shifted uncomfortably in his seat. The way she spoke to him, it was as though she was attempting to explain something simple to a small child.

"Well, you are very similar," he said awkwardly. *How did she manage to have this effect on him, as though he had been a fool?* "Same age, raised in the same household, and you are twins, of course…"

Miss Olivia's smile was wry and a little too knowing for Colin's liking. "That does not make us the same person, Your Grace."

And with that, as though he had bored her, she looked down at her embroidery, a small frown appearing on her forehead as she concentrated on her next stitch.

The whole conversation had made Colin feel rather, well, unsettled.

He had never really considered her properly. She was part of the scenery. Always there, never the focus of any conversation. They were so alike, and he had not considered it worth getting to know her. He knew Isabella. *Was that not enough?*

The only times he could ever remember hearing her speak was when they had been forced. Prevent Isabella from embarrassing herself. The sister had been most useful in distracting Isabella from her nonsense.

"Right," Colin said, unable to leave the silence there. "Well, it will be a few hours, then we can stop for luncheon, but we won't make it to Brighton in one day. We'll have to stop off at an inn, I'm afraid."

Miss Olivia looked serene. "I know. Thank you, Your Grace."

Colin blinked. "What do you mean, you know?"

It was all getting so confusing.

The twin looked at him with something far closer to a glare than a smile. "It is Isabella who has no comprehension of distances, not me. We are about fifty miles away, and with the roads in these bad conditions, there is no possibility of us getting there in one day. Not without changing the horses twice, and I doubt there will be sufficient stock of them, not with so many people journeying to London for the season. So, tomorrow then."

And without another word, her gaze fell back to her embroidery.

Colin felt as though he had been physically winded. It was the most bizarre experience he had ever had; looking at Isabella, or who could have been Isabella, but hearing some very un-Isabella-like things coming out of that pretty mouth.

"Right," he said, unnecessarily. Miss Olivia did not look up. "Understood."

"Do not worry, Your Grace, it happens to everyone."

"What do you mean?"

Miss Olivia affixed him with a rather severe look. "May I speak plainly, Your Grace? Everyone considers me just a part of Isabella. No one thinks I am myself. And then, after hearing me speak for less than five minutes, people realize we are very different people. I am not sure whether that is a comment on Isabella or myself, but there we are. I hope you can now see I am not Isabella, no matter how much I look like her."

It appeared she did not require a response.

Colin took in a slow breath as he stared at the enigma before him. *He could never have predicted that.* There was fire there and cleverness—far more intelligence than the wit he had seen in Isabella.

Perhaps this would not be the very worst carriage ride he had ever experienced.

Chapter Five

Olivia could not help it. Before she brought her fork to her mouth, she looked around nervously, stomach churning and the back of her neck prickling.

Someone was watching her. It was not possible that they could be here, sitting at an inn eating dinner, without someone spotting them. Someone would see the Duke of Larnwick was not married.

"Eat," said the duke stiffly.

Olivia turned back to their table. His plate was almost empty, His Grace ravenous. Her own was full of chicken and potatoes.

It had been a long day in the carriage, and her stomach was hungry or anxious, she was not entirely sure which. Every bone in her body ached. Olivia could not remember being this tired, which was foolishness. *What had she done but sit for eight hours!*

She had felt so useless sitting there, embroidery in hand. Every minute had taken them closer to Brighton, but what if she had been wrong? What if Isabella was not there, and all she had done was taken them on a wild goose chase while Isabella got further and further away?

It was a terrible thought, one she had not voiced to her parents nor to the duke. They had trusted her. They looked at her and saw Isabella and believed she understood her twin.

Olivia swallowed. *And there she had been, giving the duke a lecture in his carriage about how she was different!*

The scent of the roasted chicken rose, and she took a hasty mouthful.

The last thing she needed was for the news to get out. If the scandal sheets discovered Miss Isabella Lymington had not married the Duke of Larnwick, after several postponements, her reputation would be ruined. *Hers, and that of her sisters.*

All four Lymington girls would be considered unmarriageable, even with the large dowries their father had bestowed on them. It was critical they got to Brighton without being recognized, and sitting here felt like a wild and rebellious thing to do.

If they were not careful...

Olivia took another bite of her food. Thankfully, they had been placed in a corner. All they had to do was finish their meal and retire to their rooms. The duke had been careful to choose one for her on the other side of the inn, for which she was thankful.

The last thing the Lymington family needed was another scandal, on top of the one they had already experienced.

Olivia ate hurriedly. The sooner she finished, the sooner she could be upstairs alone. She had never wanted to be alone more in her entire life.

"Is the food to your liking?" The duke's words were stiff.

Olivia looked up. She had never seen a man sit so discomforted by his surroundings, *or perhaps*, she mused, *her company*.

He was a strange gentleman. At once relaxed, and then in a moment, awkward and aloof. As though he thought she was Isabella.

"Yes, it is delicious," Olivia said honestly. *The food was surprisingly good.* "I apologize for not being an adept conversationalist, Your Grace. I am tired, after...everything."

She did not explain what she meant. She did not need to.

She had spoken long into the night with her parents after the duke had left their home, and then her two younger sisters had pestered her for the details when she had gone up to bed.

There was a headache brewing in her temples, but she would not complain. *They had made good time.* Tomorrow, they would be in Brighton.

With Isabella.

"Please do not apologize," he said. "And please, call me Larnwick. You don't have to 'Your Grace' all the time. You are not here to entertain, nor defer."

"No," said Olivia instinctively. "I am here to find your bride."

Their gazes met, and a rush of heat flowed through her body. He was so irritatingly attractive, and whenever she attempted to speak naturally, as she would to any other gentleman or lady she was dining with, the words somehow sounded...well.

Flirtatious. It was not the way a young lady spoke to a gentleman, at any rate. Not when they were alone together and would be traveling alone again tomorrow.

Olivia's gaze dropped. All she had to do was finish her meal, then she could escape.

"Yes. Yes, you are," said the duke slowly. "Here's hoping it will not take too long."

Olivia nodded, not trusting her voice. She was not entirely sure she would ever be able to call him Larnwick, as though she was a friend in the club, a gentleman of his class.

Her father had been born into poverty. It was not something he was ashamed of, and so Olivia and the other Lymington girls had never considered it shameful either, but she was no fool. She knew how many of the titled classes looked at a family like her's.

Upstarts was the politest term she had heard.

"I hope you do not mind, but once we are done, I would like to retire," he said unexpectedly. "I know it may sound a little foolish, but my time alone is precious to me. It is difficult for me to relax without at least an hour in solitude. I hope you take no offense, for none is meant."

He looked genuinely concerned she would be irritated with him.

"As long as you do not take any offense when I agree wholeheartedly," she said with a nervous smile. "I am quite of your thinking, though it has often been challenging with three sisters and a Mama who likes to converse after a meal. I am…I am just the same."

Why did that sound so strange? She was different from the Duke of Larnwick. Beyond the fact he was a nobleman and a Scottish one at that, there was the fact he was betrothed to her sister. Anyone who promised to live with Isabella forever was a world apart from Olivia.

She smiled but quickly hid that expression. *It would never do for him to think that she was laughing at him.*

"And how are you finding the food, sir, madam?"

Olivia jumped. Larnwick had taken so much of her attention, she had not noticed the innkeeper, a cloth tucked into his belt and a smile on his face.

"Delicious," said Olivia hastily, hoping her one-word answer would be sufficient, and the innkeeper could then leave them alone.

"Yes, very good," said Larnwick, keeping his face low.

But their short responses were no good.

"Oh, why 'tis the Duke of Larnwick! And Miss Isabella, I should have recognized you anywhere. You always stopped here with your parents on your way to Brighton!" beamed the innkeeper, looking at each of them. "Goodness, the Duke of Larnwick and his bride in my inn! On your honeymoon, are you? Brighton?"

Olivia's stomach dropped. *Oh, blast.* This was precisely what they had hoped to avoid—why oh why had she not remembered that they had stopped here so frequently!

Though it was clear that she was not the only person who had sojourned here. As she looked up, Olivia saw Larnwick's cheeks were red, and there was a furrow in that handsome face that showed just how irritated he was that he had been recognized.

Their eyes met, the sense of panic shared between them.

What could they do? There was no point in them attempting to be someone else.

So what were they to do?

The duke and his bride, that was what the innkeeper had said. Olivia tried to think.

So the news Isabella had disappeared an hour before the wedding had not yet left London, if it had been discovered at all. That was all to the good, of course, but it did not prevent this situation from being absolutely desperate.

What was she supposed to say? She would have to correct him, and then questions after questions would pour out, and she would have to say...

"Yes, my wife," said Larnwick with a brisk smile. "We are on our way to Brighton for our honeymoon, yes. How kind of you to recognize us."

Olivia stared, unable to believe she had just heard those words coming from his mouth. *What was he thinking?* Was the man out of his mind?

What did he think he was doing?

Clearly unaware of how he had ruffled his guests, the innkeeper was nodding happily.

"Yes, yes, we get many going to Brighton stopping off here to rest their horses to save from getting stuck in the roads in the night," said the innkeeper with a broad grin. "Perfectly placed, we are, especially when the roads get bad, you wouldn't believe, Y'Grace! Why, we had one coach last week..."

The man chattered on, and Olivia used his inattention to glance at Larnwick. He looked utterly serene, which was far from how she felt. Olivia knew if she did not say something in a minute, she would scream.

"Yes, my wife. We are on our way to Brighton for our honeymoon, yes. How kind of you to recognize us."

How could he say such a thing? The Duke of Larnwick had always appeared to be a rather clever man, his engagement to Isabella notwithstanding.

So what had possessed him to lie in such a way, pretend that she, Olivia, was actually her twin sister? True, it would keep the gossips away, but not for long. Not if Isabella was spotted in Brighton. Not if they could not find her and make her marry.

Olivia gave the burden of conversation to Larnwick by taking another delicious mouthful of her chicken. He had made his bed, and now he would have to lie in it. She was not going to help him with this ridiculous fabrication!

"Well, I will leave you two lovebirds to finish your meal," said the innkeeper with a grin. "Don't keep us all up, will you!"

He chuckled as he stepped away, Olivia's chest tight with agony. That he could say such a thing, and to a duchess!

Well, she amended quickly. *A woman he thought he was a duchess.*

"What are you playing at?" she hissed at the gentleman who had put her in such a position. "What possessed you to say I was—"

"I think it was rather inspired," said Larnwick coolly. "I think it may save my reputation and Isabella's. Yours."

"I am not Isabella," said Olivia fiercely, but in a low voice. *The last thing she needed was for anyone to hear that denial.*

He leaned closer. "But don't you understand? They think you are her!"

"I am not, though."

Olivia was certain she had been cool, calm, and collected, but seeing Larnwick's response to her words told her she had not. His eyebrows raised.

The intensity of her words aside, Olivia knew she was right. She could not pretend to be Isabella for another day, all in the hope of not offending an innkeeper!

"Don't you see, though," Larnwick continued quietly. "It will not matter when we catch up with her, and that will be tomorrow if the roads are kind to us, and they are sure to be. I cannot remember when it last rained."

Olivia blinked. *Rain? Roads?* He was asking her to pretend to be the sister who always ensured she was the second choice!

"All you have to do is pretend to be her in public. I ask nothing more than that," he said, seemingly unaware of just what he was asking of her. "Both of our reputations will be saved. Won't it make a difference to all you Lymington girls to have a sister who is a duchess?"

Olivia opened her mouth to argue, but after a heartbeat of consideration, closed it.

Damn him. There was a logic to his words, even if she did not like it.

Always the second choice. It was something she thought she had learned to accept when Isabella had first been told about the coming-out ball. *Isabella's* ball.

And when Olivia had asked why it was not both of them or, more importantly, she did not have her own, what had their father said?

"Isabella is the eldest daughter, Olivia, 'tis she who receives the honor."

Never mind that the difference in age was in minutes, not years.

But no longer was she merely the second choice to Isabella; now, she would have to *pretend to be her.* It was a rather disconcerting thought, and what's more, Olivia was perfectly sure that if the roles were reversed, Isabella would never do such a thing for her. It was galling, forced to put herself in this ridiculous position just to cover her twin sister's foolishness.

She looked at him, the man who had touched her heart but had never noticed her.

He had been hurt, put in a painful position, been forced to lie, which was clearly against his nature, and why? Because Isabella had put him in an impossible position. Not just him but the entire family. All would suffer, some for the rest of their lives, if they could not rectify this.

Olivia sighed heavily. "I do not like it."

She expected the duke to commiserate with her, to exclaim he would not have asked her to do it if it was not essential, that he understood how painful it was.

He did none of those things. He shrugged. "What difference does it make?"

Olivia felt the flicker of annoyance within her and looked around herself to recall that they were in public and supposed, according to the duke's own words, to be happy newlyweds.

When she was absolutely sure that she had her temper under control, she murmured, "What difference? What difference! You have no idea what it is like to be…"

She was forced to break off what would have been, Olivia was sure, a very well-constructed and passionately delivered speech about what it was like being a twin that was constantly and consistently ignored. The innkeeper was approaching them with an apologetic smile she did not like the look of at all.

"Your Grace, Your Graces! I am sorry to say I come with an apology."

Larnwick glanced at Olivia, who shrugged theatrically. The frown she received was more than enough retribution for such rudeness.

"Apology, sir?" said the duke instead. "I do not believe anything is amiss. I cannot think what you have to apologize for."

"Ah, it was but a small mistake of course, but still, to make such an error!" said the innkeeper, wringing his hands. "But 'tis all mended now, I suppose, and where there is no real harm, I do not think His Grace will be too angry."

Olivia tried not to roll her eyes. *Was everyone this servile around him?* Did he not get bored of the bowing and scraping, the constant apologies and desperation of all to please him?

Apparently not. Larnwick merely smiled and said, "Well then, no damage done."

The innkeeper bowed his head nervously. "Yes, as I said to my wife, you must have misheard the man, His Grace, I mean. Two rooms! Certainly not, a man on his honeymoon would not require two rooms! And so it is all sorted, and you do not have to worry."

Olivia felt cold, despite the warmth of the room and the heat of the fire. Two rooms? No. This could not be what she thought it was.

"Yes, she must have misheard you," continued the innkeeper, oblivious to the distress he was causing. "Two rooms for newlyweds! Nonsense, I told her, and I have personally changed your request to ensure you have the one room, Your Grace, which I don't mind telling you is rather a blessing as we are so busy tonight!"

"Wait a moment," said Larnwick hastily, "actually, we–"

"Have a lovely evening, Y'Grace," winked the innkeeper with a surreptitious look at Olivia before he disappeared into the crowd of people who had just arrived.

Olivia's whole body had gone cold. *No, this was not happening.* This was some sort of nightmare. Perhaps she was still asleep in the carriage, not yet arrived at the inn!

She looked at Larnwick, whose lighthearted smile had disappeared. *He had certainly not predicted this consequence as a part of his ruse.*

"What are we going to do now?" hissed Olivia.

Larnwick sighed. "Oh God, I don't know." It appeared he had run out of ideas as he threw up his hands in the air. "Let's...let's just go upstairs and see what we have to work with. You never know, there could be a way to..."

His voice trailed away as Olivia gave him a sharp look. *Absolutely not!* If he had any thought of sharing a bed with her, he could stop it right now.

It was bad enough she was alone with him, worse that she was being mistaken for her twin sister, but there was absolutely no way that she would permit him to sleep beside her!

Olivia's heart sank as they ascended the stairs and saw the room they had been given. It was small, but then she had not expected much in an inn like this. It would have been perfect for one person, or perhaps two people who were very much in love.

To her great relief, she saw a small sofa pushed up against the window.

"I'll take this, then," said Larnwick heavily, dropping on the sofa. Dust flew up all around him, and he coughed as he continued, "And you take the bed."

Olivia sat on the bed. She was so tired, so ready for sleep, but desperately wished for time on her own to think about the day's events, to allow her mind to slow and steady itself.

She would certainly not get that here, not with Larnwick in the room.

Worse, how was she supposed to get undressed for bed? She had never slept in a room with a man before!

Olivia looked over at him. The duke, whether he realized it or not, was a very handsome man. She swallowed. *Some ladies would take advantage of this circumstance. Take advantage of him.*

"Look, this is not what either of us would have hoped for," said Larnwick gruffly, "but it is what it is."

Olivia nodded. *What else was there to say?*

"Tomorrow we'll find Isabella, organize the wedding, and you'll be back in London before you know it."

"I suppose," said Olivia quietly. "But before then, I will require you to turn around."

He frowned. "Why?"

Olivia's shocked look appeared to communicate far quicker than words. Larnwick's cheeks flushed, and he hastily rose from the sofa and turned to face the wall.

Olivia swallowed. *This was not what she had expected at all.* "Good night."

Chapter Six

Colin breathed out heavily, cigar smoke wafting in the early morning air mingled with the steam of his warm breath.

He had wanted a cigar the moment he had stepped into that go-dawful room last night, but there had been no opportunity to smoke while Olivia was there, and he could hardly ask her to step outside. Then, before he had known what he was doing, Colin had fallen asleep on that cursed sofa in his clothes.

He had experienced a rather nasty awakening, too, slipping off the narrow piece of furniture and slamming to the floor. Miss Olivia had screamed, of course, to be expected given the circumstances.

He supposed, he thought bitterly, *he should be grateful that no one stormed into the room to ensure his 'wife' was quite well.*

Colin was standing outside the inn, taking in the delightfully warm and pungent smoke that his cigar afforded. He should have brought a few more of these for the journey. He should have brought a whole box, but he had not expected the damn thing to be so difficult.

Go to Brighton, find his bride. How hard could it be?

With Olivia sleeping in the same room, the temptation to peek as she changed had grown ever more intense as he was forced to stare at a wall.

How many times had he attempted to kiss Miss Isabella Lymington? He had never forced himself on her, he was no rake, but still, she had been so tempting. So beautiful. And she was his betrothed, and surely there could be no harm in a kiss?

Miss Isabella had obviously thought so, and Colin had respected that. Mostly. But to have her twin sister, like her in every way just feet from him, undressing…

Well, he was not entirely made of stone. Though parts of him had been in that moment.

A few people were leaving, attempting to get on the road before first light. *The roads were going to be even worse today*, Colin thought ruefully. He should have forced Olivia to come downstairs, eat a little breakfast, and get on the road.

But he had not. She had awoken with a start, eyes wide and hair flowing down her back in that gorgeous chestnut hue, and Colin…

He swallowed, and then took another draught of his cigar. He had just stood there, looking at her. He had never seen anyone look so beautiful, so delicate, so strong. She had pierced him with a look that would have felled mountains.

It had certainly felled him. All he had managed was a strange gurgling sound, and he had then strode out of the room, down here, taking refuge in a calming smoke.

Fool. He had just had the worst sleep of his life and had probably frightened the girl out of her wits. *Isabella. Olivia. Isabella in public, Olivia when they were alone together.*

Alone together. Colin stamped his feet in the cold and tried not to think about it. He would need every ounce of self-control he possessed.

All they had to do was find Isabella and make her fulfill the promise she had given two years ago. It was not as though he was demanding something she had not given freely.

Colin's cigar was almost out, and he threw it down to the ground in disgust. He had barely had time to think about Isabella, not with Olivia so…so *present*.

Now he was alone, panic flooded into his heart. *Why had she left?* Why had she not told him how she felt? Why was it so difficult to be open? *He was supposed to be her husband!*

They could have talked, resolved it before whatever it was had overwhelmed her. She would never have taken it into her head to simply disappear like that if she had known he would have supported her, listened to her, heard her concerns.

Colin breathed in deeply and found his thoughts quickly meandered to the woman upstairs.

Olivia. He hoped she would show him a little more patience than she had hitherto afforded him. It was hardly his fault she was the second-born twin.

Olivia. She was beautiful. Well, of course she was, she was Isabella's double. The Lymington sisters were all beautiful, but the twins had been famous even in Edinburgh, where he had sojourned before his journey down to London all those years ago.

Colin smiled wryly in the early morning sun. He had been hooked before he had even met them and had sought them out as soon as he could.

One look at Isabella...

But then, could it not have been Olivia? It was hard to recall now, and he had certainly not spoken to any Lymington that first ball. The idea it could have been Olivia to first capture his attention, Olivia that had seared his heart...it was rather strange.

But he must not think of her. She would be his sister-in-law within a few days, and her similarity to his bride was a mere factor of birth.

Though he knew that, Colin was uncomfortably aware his body did not. She was doing strange things to him, this woman being so close to him. The sooner he could get away from her, return his true bride to his side, the better.

"Ah, there you are."

Colin spun around and smiled inanely at the woman stepping toward him.

"Ah, Isabella," he said loudly. "Excellent. Are you ready to depart?"

He could not help but notice the glare she gave him. "No, I am not. I have not breakfasted, and from what I can see, neither have you. Should we not—"

"I quite agree. We should get on the road immediately," Colin said loudly but with a stern look. Really, she could try to understand him. They had known each other for…no. *That was Isabella.* "I have inquired, and parcels of food have been prepared for us to consume on the road. The sooner we reach Brighton, the better."

Their gazes met, her clear, bright eyes penetrating his own. Colin swallowed. It was rather odd, but he would get used to it. It was but one day, and as soon as they were in the coach, they could forget about this subterfuge.

"Fine," she said shortly, evidently displeased with him but unable to do much about it as others left the inn to depart themselves. "Lead on, Your Gr–*dear.*"

There had never been so much venom put into one syllable, Colin thought as he opened the door of his carriage and helped her inside.

Really, he was not entirely sure what she was upset about. All she had to do was answer to whatever name was thrown at her. It was he who had the difficult job of remembering what to call her and when. She had the easy role in their little game. It was his reputation on the line, all because her twin sister could not keep her promises!

Colin pulled himself into the carriage and seated himself opposite his companion, trying to keep his breath steady. The last few thoughts had raised his temper, and he was careful not to blame the sister. *It was hardly her fault.*

Tapping the roof of the carriage, Colin handed his guest a parcel of food still warm.

"Here," he said gruffly. "I thought you would not mind. Sooner we get moving, the better."

He opened his own parcel as his mouth watered and discovered what appeared to be a meat pie. *Perfect. Hot, stodgy food.*

"And how did you sleep, Isabella?"

The look he received would have melted wax. "When we are alone, you can call me by my actual name, Larnwick. You remember it?"

Her glare was fierce, but Colin could not take her too seriously. "Oh, I am so tired, Miss Olivia, you will have to forgive me."

He took a large mouthful of the pie and felt his spirits start to restore immediately. There was nothing like a hot meal to make the world feel better all of a sudden.

It did not appear his guest was as enamored with her meal as he was, however. She had unwrapped her parcel and was looking at her pie with a look of discomfort and confusion.

"How am I supposed to eat this?"

Colin did not reply with words but simply brought his pie to his face once more and took a large bite.

Olivia stared and then laughed. "You…you have a bit of…"

Raising a finger, Colin brushed some pastry from his face and smiled. "'Tis not the most refined dining experience, I grant you, but it is delicious. Try some."

Looking at him with distrust, Olivia was too hungry to argue. She took a large bite of her warm pie, and her eyes closed in pleasure.

Colin grinned. *She really was all right, this Olivia.* He could not have imagined Isabella taking such an eager bite of a pie in any circumstance. It was strange, looking into the eyes of a woman who was, for all intents and purposes, his bride, but seeing her act in a way that was utterly contrary to the woman he knew.

"It's strange," he said quietly. "Looking at you and seeing Isabella."

He had not expected Olivia to put the pie down in its wrapper on the seat beside her and to affix him with a stare that was both serious and somewhat frightening.

"Look," she said bluntly. "I am going to be honest with you, Larnwick, far more honest than I am with most people. I think, after the last few days, you have earned it."

Colin did not know what to say, so he nodded.

Olivia looked carefully at him. "It pains me to be mistaken for Isabella."

He waited for more. "Isabella? But she is your twin sister."

She rolled her eyes as the carriage rattled along the road. "Yes, I am fully aware of that, Larnwick. You think I do not know? But I…she and I are completely different, though I am the second choice in most situations. But I am still my own person."

"I know that," protested Colin.

"Do you?" Her look was piercing, that elegant beauty he had always admired in Isabella now resplendent in Olivia. "Because I deserve to be treated as someone different, a woman with my own hopes. My own desires."

Was it her use of the word desire? Somehow, and Colin was not sure how, the temperature of the carriage had suddenly risen, and he was highly conscious of her mouth.

Olivia licked her lips, which did not help. "I just wanted to say that. I thought you deserved to know my true feelings."

"But I understand all of that," Colin protested. He was hardly some cad of one and twenty, unable to comprehend a lady wished to feel special. "I am no fool who—"

"Accidently calls me by my twin sister's name?"

The silence after Olivia's pronouncement could have been cut with a knife. Colin coughed awkwardly and sought some sort of response. *This was all getting out of hand, for no one spoke to him like this.* He was a duke.

"Look, Your Grace," said Olivia quietly. Her eyes did not waver from his. "I am doing this as a favor. I did not wish to leave my parents. It may have escaped your notice, but I am still waiting to find my match. I am doing it for my sister and you."

"For me?" Colin did not understand. What obligation did she have for his sake?

The carriage rattled over a bump and jostled them, but that could not be the reason for Olivia's flushed cheeks.

"Not you, precisely," she amended. "More…for both of you. To save your reputations. 'Tis not my reputation that is going to be ruined."

"I am not so sure," Colin countered. *He could not permit this Miss to have her way throughout the entire conversation.* "I am sure it would become difficult for you and your sisters to—how did you put it? 'Find your match', with such a stain on your sister's reputation. Your twin sister, no less."

He had not intended to be harsh, but the words had come out far more nastily than he had meant. It was not like him to be so rude to a young lady, but there was something about this woman that drew out the fire in his blood.

Besides, she did not appear too offended. In fact, she laughed. "Oh, I would not concern yourself too much, Larnwick. No one was showing much interest in me anyway. Everyone had eyes for Isabella, not me."

Olivia picked up the pie and took another bite while Colin looked at her thoughtfully. For all his bluster, he had to admit he had never entirely considered what she said.

What was it like to be a twin? To look at another person and see yourself, though not yourself? To see the small imperfections no one else sees? To watch what appears to be yourself making mistakes, worse, making a fool of yourself, and the world believing that to be you?

Colin shivered. *He would certainly not choose such a life.*

"It was just a mistake of a name," he said more softly. "And I am sorry for it."

"Yes, just a small mistake for you, but one of thousands I have been subjected to," said Olivia after swallowing a mouthful of pie. "As the younger and less beautiful Lymington twin, I am always the second choice. It is something I am learning to live with."

Colin could barely believe what he was hearing as his carriage continued to rattle along the road to Brighton. That Olivia, the woman before him who outshone almost any other woman he had ever encountered, would consider herself less beautiful!

"But…but you are identical!" he spluttered.

It was the wrong thing to say.

Olivia laughed dryly as she finished her pie and folded the wrapper in her fingertips. "Well, you might think that, but it hasn't stopped my family, our friends, and those I have never met from ensuring I know that Isabella is the more beautiful, more witty, more charming one."

Colin stared. If anyone else had said this, he would have thought they were playing for attention, but he could hear the pain in her voice. Olivia had been hurt not once, not even several times, but over the years. No wonder his small blunder had proved so painful.

"You know she was the one who had a coming-out ball?" said Olivia. "I asked for one, or even to share Isabella's, but my parents said that what they were doing was sufficient."

Colin's mouth fell open. "Wh-What? That was not fair!"

It was more than that; it was ridiculous. Twin sisters not being given the same celebration as they came out into society?

"Did you know that Isabella chooses all our gowns, the styles, the fit, the fabric, the color, and the dressmakers just make a second for me?" said Olivia in that same painfully controlled conversational tone. She picked at the sleeve of the gown she was wearing. "I would never choose something like this."

Colin did not know what to say. He was hardly a sartorial expert. "You don't even choose your own clothes?"

Olivia shook her head. "I don't choose anything, Larnwick. I am the second twin, the second choice, and that means I *have* the second choice. It is Isabella who decides which invitations we accept, which balls we attend, whether or not I wear the gold earbobs or she does... Isabella has all the power."

"But why do you put up with it?" Colin found himself asking—*a personal question indeed, but then she had been the one to open herself so freely.*

Olivia frowned as though she did not understand. "What would I do? Where would I go? That is how it has always been, and until her marriage, it always will be. That is why I do not wish to be called Isabella, except when necessary. I am tired of it. *I am not her.*"

Colin had never felt such guilt before. Her words had greatly affected him, and though they fell into silence as the carriage continued on, he could not stop thinking about her words.

Now he understood. Now the painful expression when he had first called her Isabella, before the innkeeper, made sense.

"I did not know," he said quietly. "You must forgive my ignorance."

Olivia examined him for a moment before saying softly, "I do not blame you for the injury caused me over the years. You had no knowledge of it, but now you do, and I urge you to consider your words more carefully. Besides, I am the second choice here, even now."

Colin's heart turned cold. *Surely she did not mean...*

"Here I am, bait to lure out the woman you really want," said Olivia lightly, bitterness only just detectable. "An informant to hunt her down. You had no desire to spend time with me, but that is so often the way. They wish to converse with Isabella and end up with me."

"Well, if 'tis any consolation," he said gently, "I think you just as pretty as your sister."

He had expected thanks, perhaps a blush. What he received was an ironic eye roll.

"You expect me to be grateful? Once again, the second choice.

Why can I only be pretty compared to her, to Isabella? Why cannot anyone consider me pretty on my own merits?"

Colin had not expected such ingratitude and found his temper flaring. "Do not lay all this at my door, Miss Olivia! Your sister was the Lymington your parents offered me and..."

"So you did not even think for yourself?" shot back Olivia. "You did not consider your future wife, the mother of your future children, someone worth talking to before you decided to marry her?"

Colin gaped, utterly lost for words. No one had accused him of such negligence in considering his future bride before. He was a duke! He was fortunate indeed he had not been maneuvered into an arranged marriage as poor Orrinshire had been. *Though from memory, he had never actually gone through with it.*

Colin looked at Miss Olivia, and as his temper died away, he wondered why he had not considered these things before. They were so obvious when Olivia spoke. He opened his mouth to admit that, but he was interrupted before he could even start.

"Look," she said brusquely, "I should not have spoken so openly. Let's just find her. Then the two of you can live your lives in Scotland, and I can finally live my own. Separately."

Colin blinked, again blindsided by her honesty. He had always assumed—with little evidence, in hindsight—that twins were naturally close. Closer than siblings ever usually were.

But now he had come to spend more than five minutes in her company, he found, to his astonishment, that it was Olivia who was the thoughtful, intelligent one. Not Isabella.

"Olivia," he began hesitantly.

Olivia did not meet his gaze. She pulled a book out of her reticule and disappeared behind it.

She was right. What had her father said only two days ago?

"Her sister, an exact match. Why not marry her?"

Yes, a second choice, but perhaps, if he had been smart, he would have chosen her.

Colin shook his head. *No, it was madness to think in such a way*. He could not think like that now. He had to focus on what this journey was really about.

Isabella, his betrothed. He had to find her. Before he made a more significant mistake.

Chapter Seven

It was possible, if one was very careful, to gently move a small flap in the carriage side that allowed the air of the road into the small interior space. Olivia had noticed it when she had first embarked, all the way back in London—which felt like an age ago now.

She had not been interested in it then. *What need she for the smell of the road?*

But now, a familiar sight had appeared through the dark gloom of evening, her fingers hastened, untying it to allow in the air of the road.

The salty air.

"Brighton," she breathed.

She did not need to see the town to know it was there. Not with that sharp freshness on the air, that delicious blend of seaweed and outgoing tide. She would know it anywhere.

Within minutes, the night was pitch black. The hour was not that late, yet the time of year meant the sun had entirely disappeared, though they were almost there.

Brighton. The town where she had, no, she must not think of it. It was not painful, exactly, but it was hardly the sort of memory she wished to revisit.

Especially not in his company. *Larnwick.*

"Brighton," she breathed, almost unable to help herself.

She had thought she would be so happy here. This was the place where all her dreams were supposed to come true, where she would honor her family and become…

But it was not to be. Isabella had made sure of that.

Olivia swallowed. She was not going to allow bitter memories from the past to affect her. What had been a one-day journey in the summer, summers full of sunshine and heat and laughter, had taken two full days on the road in Larnwick's carriage, and she was exhausted.

The sooner she could get out of this carriage and into her own bed, the better.

It was not just the travel which had tired her. No, it was being seated in a small rattling box with Larnwick that had made her, in turn, rattled.

She had been more open with him than with anyone in years, and in a way, she knew her parents would have disapproved.

But somehow, she knew he would not tell anyone what she had shared.

He was a good man, as well as a handsome one, so it was completely natural that she would feel…*warm* toward him.

Olivia chastised herself. She had to be careful. The last thing she needed was to start to care *too much* for the man. He was Isabella's betrothed, and she was the only reason that they were here.

He was not interested in her. Larnwick had made this journey to retrieve his bride.

He has already been offered you, Olivia reminded herself, cringing at the memory of her father's words.

"Her sister, an exact match. Why not marry her?"

If he had any interest in her whatsoever, he would have perked up at that point, but he had not. His only interest was in securing Isabella.

"Ah, we're here."

Olivia smiled. If she was not mistaken, Larnwick had slipped into a slumber in the last hour of their journey, though she had judiciously ignored the slight snoring noise that may or may not have emitted from him during that time.

"Yes, we are in Brighton," said Olivia. "One of my favorite places in the world. Goodness, to live here or even just spend summers here would be quite something."

Larnwick glanced at the window, utterly black. "I am not sure I see the attraction, but you come alive when you talk about it. You have been here often?"

"Every summer for the last few years," Olivia replied. She had to be careful. *They could get very close, if they were not careful, to the topic of...*

"Indeed," nodded Larnwick in the gloom of the carriage. "How pleasant. You must have had some good times here."

Olivia's face fell, hidden by the darkness.

Good times. Yes, there had certainly been good times. Olivia could not deny it, and yet they had all been subsumed by the actions a certain twin sister had taken.

She swallowed. She had come to peace with what Isabella had done, or at least, she had thought she had. No one could expect a perfect life with absolutely no disappointments, and in many ways, Olivia had lived a charmed life.

Except for that summer. That week, where she had thought her life was going in one direction, and instead...

She was not going to think of it. Not that she cared for him now. *But at the time...*

"It is late," she said, desperate to shift the conversation. "I had not believed it would take us this long to arrive."

Larnwick sighed. "Yes. Though I wish to find Isabella immediately, I think we would do well to settle in a hotel of some sort first, to ensure we have somewhere to stay the night. We cannot have you sleeping in the carriage!"

He laughed, and Olivia smiled. *Yes, that would undoubtedly be discomforting, though mainly because he would be in here with her.*

A traitorous flicker of hope leapt in Olivia's heart and was instantly quelled.

One last evening. That was all she had with Larnwick. It was a heady, jealous feeling. He belonged to Isabella, and in a strange way,

Olivia felt as though she had stolen him from her.

All she was doing was setting herself up for more misery, and she had certainly had her fair share of that in Brighton.

She had to remember what they were here for. *Isabella.*

A sad smile crept over her lips. *Of course it was about Isabella. It always was about her.*

"Yes, right," she said aloud. "Well, from memory, there is a rather large hotel just down the main road along the beach. I do not think it has ever been full, from what I can recall. You never know, we may even find Isabella there."

Larnwick opened the flap to speak to the driver, and as he did so, Olivia attempted to gather her spirits.

The carriage came to a rather abrupt halt, and Olivia had to put her hands out to stop herself from falling forward.

Something soft was underneath them, and only when Larnwick coughed and the soft thing moved did Olivia realize what she was touching.

"Are you all right there?"

"Yes, yes, fine," she said hastily, removing her hands and thanking God the darkness hid her scarlet cheeks. "Thank you."

She had almost thrown herself onto him!

Olivia took in a deep breath. She could not allow this foolishness to continue. She was one and twenty, and she was more than old enough to control herself!

Just because the temptation to throw herself back into Larnwick's arms was strong...

"Here, take my hand."

There in the carriage doorway was Larnwick's hand, waiting to assist her.

She swallowed. The sooner this adventure, for want of a better word, was over, the better. She was only starting to upset herself with all these fanciful thoughts.

"Th-Thank you," she stammered.

All she had to do was reach out and take his hand. If only she was wearing gloves!

How long they stood there, she could not tell. Her hand was in his, her chest rising rapidly, trying to catch the breath it had lost. There was something in his eyes, a look she had not seen before. Larnwick's expression was strange, intensely focused on her in a way it never had before.

And then it was over. The duke dropped her hand and turned to look up at the hotel.

"This is the one you meant? The Old Ship Hotel?"

Olivia could not reply, she was too busy attempting to force air back into her lungs. *What had just happened?* The moment they had shared, far too intense for words, had been but a split second, and yet it had gone on for what seemed like forever.

"Olivia?"

Hearing her name on his lips did not help, and she swallowed twice to ensure her throat was sufficiently prepared to speak. "Yes," she whispered.

It was odd, being here after so many years. *What could have possessed her to recommend this very hotel where she had found…*

It at least made sense. Isabella had already proven that she had run here before, desperate to be hidden. And she was a creature of habit, and none knew that better than Olivia. Her twin sister walked along the same paths she always did, unable to help herself.

They would find her here or in the Castle Inn. Then this whole façade would be over.

"Are you quite well?" Larnwick said, making Olivia stumble a step back.

"Well?"

He nodded, his gaze raking over her face. "Yes, well. You seem a little annoyed is the only word I can think of."

Olivia forced a smile. She would not be the one to crack under the pressure of this rather strange adventure.

"Of course I am well," she said lightly. "Just...a little tired. Let us go in."

It was a relief to stand in the hallway of the hotel with others around them, the hustle and bustle of Brighton filling her senses rather than Larnwick.

He was so masculine. So physical, so tall. Olivia could not think of the words to best describe him. All she knew was that her senses were utterly overwhelmed by him, and all she could do was step back as he spoke to the hotel clerk and hope her frantically beating heart and tense shoulders would calm themselves.

Brighton was evidently starting to fill up. There were people milling about, coming in and out of the hotel, with boxes and bags and trunks. Ladies with feathers in their hair were leaving to attend some sort of party. Footmen were scurrying in and out in the hotel's livery, taking messages, carrying things, guiding guests in and out of various doors.

It was a hive of activity, and as Olivia took a seat and allowed Larnwick to organize their rooms, the busyness somehow calmed her, slowed her thoughts.

The world had continued. It had been hard to imagine on the road, Larnwick's presence so intoxicating. As though they were in their own private world, where no one else existed.

But that was not true. The world had continued without a Larnwick wedding, almost as though it did not matter. The whole thing was ridiculous, now that she considered it.

Larnwick turned and pointed her out to the hotel clerk. Olivia smiled briefly, but he turned back to the desk without a second glance.

Olivia's smile faded. She knew she did not look exactly her best. It was difficult when on the road to look anything close to one's best, and she had the added disadvantage of almost no sleep after being forced to share a room with the man her sister was supposed to be marrying.

But they had arrived. Road-weary and tired, but in Brighton. Later this evening, their ordeal would be over, Isabella would be found, and she could return to London.

Well. Olivia was not entirely sure what she would do once Isabella and Larnwick had married and departed to Scotland. Wait to see if anyone would ask for her hand, she supposed.

"I have good news and bad news," announced Larnwick as he stepped over to her.

Olivia rose hurriedly. "Bad news?"

There was a strange and rather discomforting smile on his face. "Did I say bad news?"

She tried not to look stern. "You did indeed, Your Grace."

"Well, this delightful man here has surmised we are newlyweds," Larnwick said brightly as the hotel clerk rushed toward them with a sycophantic smile. "And so he has very kindly given us the best room in the place."

Olivia's heart sank. "Room?"

Not again. Not after she had spent all day thinking about how much she wished to be alone. Now she would have to suffer, well, not precisely suffer. *Endure.* His presence was doing something strange to her, that moment with her hand just one amongst many.

Colin Vaughn, the Duke of Larnwick, did something strange to her. Olivia swallowed. She did not understand it, and she would not until she had time to herself. *And now they were to be forced to spend another night…together?*

"Ah, what a kind thought," she said hastily.

The hotel clerk beamed. "This way, Your Grace…"

He stuck out a hand, and Olivia waited for Larnwick to step forward. It was only when the two men looked at her did she realize he was referring to her.

"Oh, yes," she said a little self-consciously. "Right. Please lead on, sir."

It seemed to take forever, going through the corridors up to the best room in the hotel. Olivia looked around it as the hotel clerk babbled about extra pillows and saw with relief that there was a large sofa to one side of the room.

Well, at least one of them would not have such a discomforting evening.

After a murmured conversation with the hotel clerk, which resulted, from what Olivia could see, in an exchange of coin from the duke to the man, they were left alone.

Olivia sat heavily on the bed. "Thank you," she said stiffly.

"No, I should be the one thanking you," said Larnwick, leaning against the wall by the door and examining her closely. "You have taken a big risk to come here with me and lie for me. I know plenty of ladies would not have even considered doing half of what you have done for me, and I am grateful."

Olivia smiled awkwardly. "'Tis the least I can do."

"No, no, it's not," he said, straightening up and taking a step forward. "You are truly an impressive woman, and I salute you."

Was it so obvious her cheeks were red? It was all Olivia could do to keep her face calm, however, when the duke put out his hand.

He…he wanted to shake her hand? But she was no gentleman!

"Isn't…isn't this a bit formal?" she said uncomfortably, leaving his hand untouched.

Larnwick shrugged. "I would shake the hand of a man, and you've been as good as one."

She could not help but laugh as she rose to her feet. "Praise indeed."

Taking his hand, somehow, shifted the entire world. Olivia had not taken a step away from the bed, but at the same time, there was a hefty pull in her navel toward the duke who stood before her. As though gravity had shifted.

There was something about him. Something delicious, wonderful, forbidden, and tainted. It was something Olivia wanted desperately, but she knew she must not have.

It was too painful and yet too sweet.

Only when she realized that she had leaned forward did Olivia come to her senses. *What was she doing?*

Olivia almost laughed. Everyone thought she was Isabella. *His wife.* Though it was a delightful lie to indulge in within the privacy of her heart, it could not be. That was not the story she would be given.

She pulled away. "Right, Isabella."

Larnwick blinked. "Isabella?"

It was all Olivia could do not to laugh. "Yes, Isabella. Your bride. You did inquire whether she was here?"

The duke nodded. It appeared speech was, at this moment, beyond him.

Olivia tried not to think that he had experienced something of the same pull that she had and continued. "Then I think she will be at the Castle Inn. We used to go there when we were young, it's very small, but she may have booked a…"

She stopped herself, but Larnwick was quicker than she gave him credit for.

"You mean you think she planned this?"

Olivia swallowed. "I will not lie to you, Larnwick. Yes. Perhaps."

Why were they standing so close to each other? Olivia's thoughts were muddled by the headiness of his presence, but one idea made it through. If her suspicion was correct, Isabella had never intended to go through with the marriage.

The duke, however, seemed to take it all in his stride. "And is this place close by?"

Olivia nodded. "On this very street."

Larnwick moved to the door. "Then there is no time like the present."

It took but a few minutes to descend to the street. Olivia tried to take in every detail. This would be her last few minutes with him.

As they stepped out into the darkness of the street, he took her arm, causing heat to flush through her body.

Before she could say anything, they were standing outside the

Castle Inn.

"Do...do you want me to come in with you?" Olivia asked softly.

Larnwick glanced at her, and there were so many unsaid words in that glance that Olivia almost gasped. *It was as though...well...*

"Yes, please," he murmured.

As they stepped inside, a clerk rushed forward. "I am sorry, sir, we have no rooms at present available for—"

"I am seeking...an acquaintance of mine," said Larnwick stiffly. "A Miss Isabella Lymington."

The clerk blinked and then turned his confused gaze to Olivia. "Well, no, sir. She is standing there, I presume. You mean her twin, do you not?"

Olivia bit her lip and glanced at Larnwick, who widened her eyes.

She had to make light of this. *She could not allow the gossip rumors to spread that the Duke of Larnwick was hunting for his wife.*

"My dear, you do tease the man something awful," she said with a light tap on Larnwick's chest. "He means my twin, of course, Miss Olivia."

The clerk's smile was enough for Olivia. *She knew it. Isabella had taken the room under her name, under the name of Miss Olivia Lymington.*

Well, it wouldn't be the first time...

"Yes, your sister was here," said the clerk. "But I am afraid she left early this morning. You have missed her by only a few hours."

Olivia glanced up at Larnwick, whose jaw tightened before he said, "And you have no idea where she went."

"On the contrary, I know precisely where she went," said the clerk with pride. "Bath, Y'Grace."

Her feet were tired, her shoulders were heavy, and Olivia needed a good meal. They were not going to catch up with Isabella if they left now, she knew that. Time to return to their hotel and suffer another night together.

"Well then," she said brightly to Larnwick. "Time for dinner."

Chapter Eight

Colin allowed his fork to drop to his plate with a clatter. "No, I cannot eat another bite. Do not tempt me!"

The laugh from his dining companion was sweet and light.

"Well, I absolutely could," said Olivia, smiling down regretfully at her empty plate. "But then, I mustn't."

"Mustn't? Mustn't is an awfully strong word from a young lady like yourself," Colin found himself teasing, his stomach tied in knots for a reason that had to be due to the large meal they had just enjoyed. "I do not believe young ladies should say such things."

And she laughed. *Oh, he knew how to make her laugh.* Colin smiled as he watched her. It was late, and when he teased her, a light shone in her eyes that he had never seen before.

When he teased Olivia. His sister-in-law to be.

Colin took a gulp of wine from his glass. *He needed to behave himself.* What would Mr. and Mrs. Lymington say if they saw them like this?

Flirting.

No, surely not. Colin had never flirted with Miss Olivia. He was just…teasing.

"No, that was quite enough cake for me," said Olivia, delicately placing her fork down.

"Why, watching your figure?" Colin found himself saying. *Damn, it was like he could not help himself.* There was something about her that drew it out of him. A sense that as long as she was smiling, as long as he could make her laugh, everything would be well.

Olivia giggled. "No, I am attempting not to spend all my father's money! I could eat another two of those cakes, but do not tempt me. I will eat him out of house and home!"

Their laughter echoed through the restaurant, and Colin only remembered they were supposed to be keeping a low profile when he saw another table turn their heads irritably to stare at them.

Only then did he notice. The chocolate cake had been delicious, decadent even, with a rich cream filling and strawberries adorning the sides. There was a small amount of that chocolate filling in the corner of Olivia's mouth. Now that Colin had noticed it, he could not look away. Her mouth. Her delicate lips, soft and welcoming and...

"What is wrong?" Olivia said. Her laughter had gone. "Is there—"

"Just a small amount of chocolate," said Colin. His voice croaked, and he had to cough to give it strength to continue. "Just...just there. In the corner of your mouth."

He could not say lips. For some reason, his ability as a gentleman to say something as innocent as 'lips' was utterly diminished.

Olivia raised her napkin to her mouth and removed the chocolate with a smile. "Saving some for later!"

Colin smiled. *God, this was pleasant.* He could not remember the last time he had sat with a lady and laughed, really laughed. He had not been so comfortable with anyone.

Was...was this what it should have been like with Isabella?

It was a treacherous thought, but Colin could not help it. Isabella was nice, that was true. Beautiful, certainly, and clever in her own way. But there was little warmth in her. You could give all your attention to her, and she just took it, giving nothing back.

But Olivia...she was a mirror. A mirrored reflection of her twin sister, but also a mirror in company. When others were short and fractious, so was she. When he was cheerful and charming, so was she.

And when he held her hand and wished to pull her into his arms and kiss her senseless...

Colin coughed again, as though that would dislodge the thought from his mind. *He should never have even entertained it at the time, let alone dwell on it later.* That was not what gentlemen did, ravish the lips of ladies who had trusted you on a journey to find their sister.

"Goodness, you are thinking deep thoughts," said Olivia lightly, taking a sip of her wine. "What is going on in that mind of yours, Larnwick?"

Larnwick. He had asked her to call him that, and in a way, it was pleasant. For some reason, Colin was overwhelmed with the desire to have his first name spoken on her lips.

"I would offer a penny for them, if I had one on me," Olivia said with a quiet smile. "You will have to trust me that I am good for the money. After all, I came into my fortune this year when I turned one and twenty."

Colin smiled weakly. *God, if she only knew what was rattling through his mind.* He was not sure she would ever be able to tell her what treacherous thoughts were going through his mind. He would rather die first, for it would be a traitor's death.

He was supposed to be thinking about Isabella, off to Bath without a soul to protect her. She was the one who should be crowding his thoughts, and instead…

Colin looked at Olivia, who smiled. *Instead, Olivia.* Had he…God, it was awful to even entertain the thought, but had he made the wrong choice?

Had he chosen the wrong twin?

Was Isabella as good-natured underneath all the bluster and nonsense, or was he about to travel halfway across the country, *again*, to chase after a woman who had no intention of marrying him and who he was starting to realize was not right for him?

"You do look very serious, Larnwick, if not a little unhappy," said Olivia, her words breaking through his thoughts. "You…you would tell me if there was something I had done to offend, wouldn't you?"

"No, you have done nothing wrong."

He must push all thoughts of Olivia as anything other than his sister away. He had chosen Isabella, and when he had been most desperate to break the engagement and simply disappear back to Scotland, he had chosen to stay.

Now he had to pick the most gentlemanly path and not tempt her. *Not tempt himself.*

"I was thinking," he began, without any real idea of where he was going, and was immediately saved by a man approaching them with a rather serious look and dressed in the hotel's livery.

"And that," said Olivia quietly, "I would say is the hotel manager. Oh, Lord."

Oh Lord indeed, thought Colin. He recognized the type; the sort of man who was desperately eager to please and evidently nervous that the two finely dressed guests, who some whispered were the Duke and Duchess of Larnwick, were happy.

"Your Graces," the man said, bowing so low his nose almost touched their table. "My name is Mr. Ferryweather, and I am honored to have you staying with us on your honeymoon."

Colin looked over the prostrate man not yet risen from his bow to Olivia.

"Yes, yes, very good," said Colin gruffly.

Mr. Ferryweather straightened up and inclined his head to Olivia. "Miss Isabella, what a delight to have you return to our establishment. And the food was to your satisfaction? And the wine? The wine is good? If it is not to your taste, I can quite easily send out for—"

"No, no, the wine is fine, the food is good," interrupted Colin. *Anything to get this man to leave them alone.*

Besides, he was not typically in the business of complimenting anyone. That was not his style. It was expected that everything should be perfect, and that was the minimum level a man of his rank should receive.

"Oh, sir, 'tis most wonderful, and we are grateful for the little attentions we have received," said Olivia to Colin's surprise. "I must say, the place has only improved under your tender care. The drapes over the curtains in the rooms, they are new, are they not?"

Colin watched as Olivia managed to tangle the man into raptures of his own making. She smiled and laughed and made Mr. Ferryweather blush with the little niceties she trotted out.

Colin said nothing but watched her.

Olivia was quite different. It was embarrassing now to look back a few days when he had so vehemently tried to convince her that they were the same.

The same!

"You remembered!" cried Mr. Ferryweather in fits of delight. "My goodness, not many of patrons recall that summer. Yes, the band was excellent, but I was most pleased with..."

Colin watched Olivia smile, nod, respond prettily to something the man said. Yes, the Lymington twins were different, more different than he had known.

Isabella was selfish, always interested in how everyone saw her, but Olivia was more interested in others. She asked questions that were meaningful and, more importantly, actually cared about the answers! *If he could have his time again...*

But no, that simply wasn't a way he could think. He had to learn to be happy with the sister he had, if he could ever catch up with her!

"—leave you to finish your wine," Mr. Ferryweather was saying, leaving after a bow.

It was only then Olivia noticed how closely Colin was examining her. "Please do not tell me I have just spent five minutes conversing with Mr. Ferryweather with chocolate on my face."

"What? Oh, no," said Colin hastily, seeking to reassure her. "I was just marveling at your conversational skills, that was all."

Was that a flush? A flush of pleasure at his words? Why was he seeking that at all?

"No, that is not entirely it," said Olivia slowly.

Colin shifted in his seat. "You think I am lying to you?"

He had expected her to laugh at the jest, but instead, she shook her head slowly. "No, you have never lied to me, Larnwick. But I think you are considering something far more serious."

Colin laughed. He could not think how else to respond; was he to admit that he had been considering her as an alternative bride?

"Isabella?" Olivia said quietly with a sympathetic look. "I am sorry we did not manage to catch up with her in time. She is but one day ahead of us, which I suppose is a small mercy."

Colin swallowed.

"Yes, that is good," he said quietly, finding no joy at the thought of catching up with Isabella in the morning. *Not when he had an excellent alternative before him.*

No, he could not think that way! He needed to get a hold of himself. Olivia would certainly not accept his affections if he offered them. *Probably.*

"Do you remember the first time we ever met?" Colin found himself saying.

Olivia leaned back in her chair and nodded. "Yes. Yes, I do. We were at Lady Romeril's ball, were we not?"

Colin nodded. "It seems like an age ago."

"That is because it was over two years ago, and nothing much else has happened since," quipped Olivia with a grin. "Yes, you were introduced to us, by who I cannot remember now, and you said—"

"Which of the pretty Lymington sisters will dance with me?" said Colin with a laugh. "God, I was awful then. And you said—"

"Everyone," Olivia cut in with a wry smile, "dances with Isabella."

They sat in silence for a moment. Colin wanted to speak. *Did he regret that moment?* Did she, Olivia, regret pushing her twin sister forward at that moment?

"'Tis still true, you know," said Olivia softly, breaking the silence. "Most of the gentlemen who end up dancing with me finish by thanking Miss Isabella Lymington."

A smile remained on her lips, but it was sad now. Colin wished to wipe it away, force the world to see the incredible woman that sat before him.

"But I am used to it now."

He shook his head and found himself saying, "I will admit, it feels madness now that anyone would not be able to tell you apart. You are so different, your mannerisms, your preferences. Your priorities. How you treat people, like Mr. Ferryweather."

Olivia's eyes had widened. "You…you noticed that?"

"I am noticing a lot of things about you," Colin said quietly.

The restaurant was starting to empty now; the hour was drawing late, and there were plenty of yawns amongst the patrons retiring to their rooms.

But Colin could not countenance rising from his seat now. *Not when his conversation had become so…so interesting.*

"I admit myself astonished," said Olivia softly, her gaze not leaving his own. "Most people cannot tell the difference between us. Even some long-standing friends, even our parents at times cannot."

"I can," said Colin.

The intensity of his gaze, his inability to look anywhere else, and the desire that was surely visible to her was making her blush.

Damnit man, you needed to control yourself! But Colin could not. He wanted her, wanted her in a way he had never desired the sister. Isabella was all very well, but she was a pale imitation of the real thing as he sat here, gazing at Olivia.

He had spent the last two years so focused on Isabella, trying to get her to go through with this wedding, trying to *make* her marry him, that he had paid no attention to the sister.

He should have done. He had before him a far superior woman, and he had not understood this until it was too late.

"I…I had considered breaking off my engagement to your sister."

Olivia's eyes widened. "You did?"

Colin nodded. *It was madness, telling her this, but not to do so felt like lying now, after she had been so open with him.*

"I was tired of it, all the delays, all the pontification," he said heavily. "I felt desperate to be free. I…I thought of just writing a letter to your father and leaving for Scotland."

"Just like Isabella did."

Colin laughed dryly. "Yes, it does all feel rather coincidental, doesn't it? It was only when she did that that I realized she had to marry me. I have waited too long to be trifled with."

Did she understand? Colin thought he saw a flicker of comprehension in her eyes. Yes, this was the safest way to tell her he was determined to marry her, Isabella, even if…even if his better judgment now suggested an alternative course of action.

"I…I am so tired, all of a sudden," said Olivia, rising to her feet. "I think I will—"

"Yes, of course," Colin said hastily, following suit. "Yes. Sleep."

It took but a moment for them to enter their room, and as they did so, Colin looked with dread at the sofa.

"I do think that I should take the sofa, really," said Olivia. She closed the door behind her and leaned against it.

Colin shook his head. "Absolutely not. I would never dream of such a thing. I am the one who should be thanking you on bended knee and apologizing too for taking you away from Brighton where you were. You are so happy."

"I do not mind," said Olivia, taking a step forward. "I would do anything to make you happy. I meant…"

Her voice trailed away, and it was only then that Colin realized why she had agreed to come with him on this foolish journey in the first place.

She had a liking for him. There was no other explanation. What woman would agree to risk her reputation to accompany a man on a journey like this?

It was too much. The desire he had pushed aside over the last few days rose, and there was nothing he could do to prevent what happened next.

Colin stepped forward, pulling Olivia into his arms, and kissed her hard on the mouth.

He had expected her to struggle, to be surprised at the liberty he had taken with her, and to push him away.

But no. Olivia wanted him just as much as he wanted her, it appeared, for she sank into his arms and wrapped her own around his neck, pulling him closer. Her lips parted, welcoming him in, and Colin almost groaned aloud with the sweetness of her, the softness. She was perfect, and they were perfect together, matched as though betrothed from birth. This was far greater an experience, far more pleasure than he had ever found with Isabella.

The thought of his betrothed made him pull away. Colin stared into Olivia's eyes, unsure how to break the silence.

What was it her father had said?

"Her sister, an exact match. Why not marry her?"

But Olivia had shared her thoughts on that matter in the carriage.

"I am the second twin, the second choice, and that means I have the second choice..."

Colin swallowed, still tasting Olivia's lips on his own. She had always played second fiddle to her sister, but now perhaps was the time to usurp her, to take her place in the wedding? *Could he do it? Would the world censure him as a madman?*

"Olivia," he breathed.

For the first time, Colin considered it seriously. He and Olivia could be happy, he was almost sure of it. She was beautiful, clever, witty, and far more kind than her sister had ever showed herself to be. He looked deep into her eyes and saw Olivia, not Isabella.

"Colin," she whispered.

No. No, this was not right! The wedding between him and Isabella had been planned for months, years! It was Isabella they were hunting down.

"God, I am so sorry," he said and stepped back.

"No, no, I am the one who should apologize."

"Don't know what came over me," blustered Colin, knowing full well what had just come over him. "Too much wine for both of us."

"Yes, yes, that must be it," Olivia said hastily. She turned away and moved over to the bed. "Time for sleep, I think."

They did not say another word to each other that evening, and Olivia blew out the lamp within ten minutes. That did not prevent Colin, however, from lying wide awake on the sofa for many hours.

What would have happened if he had not thought of Isabella at that moment? Would he even now be in that bed with Olivia?

Chapter Nine

OLIVIA TOOK ONE last, deep breath of the salty air as she looked out over the beach to the ocean. She had been unable to see it in the dark when they had arrived last night. It had almost been possible to believe it was not there.

It looked chilly, a dark grey under a heavy sky. Winter did Brighton no favors, in her opinion. Summer was when the place came alive. Olivia knew most people, like her sister, preferred the balls and the parties to the bathing and sunburned skin the summer brought.

Olivia closed her eyes and felt the rough wind against her skin. There were so many happy memories here; dancing along the sand with her sisters, laughing as gusts whipped it up above them. Splashing in the sea with her mother. The card games they would play in the evenings, sun still up, picking at sweetmeats and cakes until their father would order them all to bed.

Happy times. *But not all happy times. When he…when he had…*

What would her life have been like if Harold had decided to come to be loyal to her instead of her sister?

"Ready to be off?"

Olivia smiled rigidly at the gentleman beside her by the coach.

Colin Vaughn, Duke of Larnwick. It was a miracle she could look at him after what she had done with him. What line she had crossed.

"Almost," she said softly, turning back to the sea.

The sea. It never changed, never betrayed her, never made her feel such things that she knew were not permitted, not allowed.

Yet it felt right that she was here in Brighton with him. It was remarkable to her, and he was becoming more special to her with every passing moment. *Dangerously so*. If he had not pulled away from her last night, after that intoxicating and confusing kiss, then…

Well. Olivia was not entirely sure what would have happened. She knew the ways of love, at least in theory. She had been told at a certain age, and though Isabella had done a fair amount of giggling over their mother's words, the two of them in that bedchamber, with the bed before them, the entire hotel already thinking they were making love…

"You will be back before you know it," said Colin briskly.

Olivia nodded without replying. *How could she, when she did not trust her voice?*

Her first kiss, and with the man who was going to marry her sister. Now she was stuck in this nightmare of a transgression, unable to take it back!

There had been a moment as they had breakfasted in the hotel when he had looked at her and said her name in such a wistful, soft manner that Olivia had almost melted on the chair.

Her emotions may have poured out of her in such a shameful display that the duke would have been forced to do something drastic.

Like marry her.

Olivia flushed at the very thought. No, that would not be the end of this ridiculous tale. She needed to get some distance from him. As soon as they found Isabella and their wedding was over, she could leave this all behind her.

Leave him behind her.

"You know, I have only been to Brighton a handful of times," said Colin, interrupting her thoughts. "I have never really fallen in love with the place. Too busy. Too crowded."

Olivia smiled. "You are not the only one, but that is usually because people have spent time here in the winter months. Tell me, have you ever been here in summer?"

"No."

Olivia could feel his gaze, but she did not give in to the temptation to look at him. She would not permit it. She had to be in control, even if he was not.

"Well then," she said lightly. "You have not seen it at its best."

"No," he said softly. "I have not. I have not fallen in love with Brighton."

It was such a scandalous thing to say that Olivia was not entirely sure at first whether she had heard him correctly. *Surely he had not...he was not suggesting...*

No. Colin Vaughn, the Duke of Larnwick, was not in love with her. It was time to shift this conversation onto the only person who could stop this sort of nonsense.

"You will have to come back here with Isabella," Olivia said cheerfully. "Once you are married."

Whether it was Isabella's name or the reminder of his impending marriage, she was not sure either way that her words were sufficient to remind the duke of his place. He said not another word, but he did drag his gaze away and toward the sea.

Olivia took a deep breath. She could stand here forever. Not touching, not close enough.

"We had better get into the carriage," Colin said with a sigh. "I do not wish to lose any more time. Would you like a hand?"

"No. I mean, thank you," said Olivia hurriedly, relieved she had taken the precaution of wearing gloves.

He helped her into the carriage and said bracingly, "She cannot be far off now."

Olivia nodded as she settled into the now all too familiar seat. Of course, the conversation and their attention had turned back to the reason they were even together, Isabella. She had brought them together, and once they found her, she would rip them apart.

"I must admit, I am becoming a little sick of the sight of the interior of this carriage," she said with what she hoped was a laugh. "And I suppose you will be getting sick of me, too!"

Colin settled himself opposite her but did not laugh. "I cannot imagine ever being sick of you, Olivia. If I may call you by your first name."

She nodded. It was difficult to ignore the memory of that kiss only hours before. Now they were happily ensconced inside, Olivia found her mind drifting to it again. The way he had stepped toward her, fire in his eyes...and those same eyes were examining her now.

They were alone, would be for at least another day. Just as they had been in the bedchamber last night when they succumbed to whatever feelings had been stirred up by their conversation, by the wine, by...

Olivia shivered. Even here, dressed formally in her gown and traveling cloak, and the duke dressed in his breeches, shirt, waistcoat, frockcoat, greatcoat, so many layers between each other...

And yet. Yet she could still feel the tension in the air as the carriage rattled off, along the road out of Brighton and toward Bath. They would not be disturbed now for hours, just the two of them here. *No one would know.*

It took all her determination to think of something else. Her embroidery took most of her attention, and as she was working around a difficult portion of a petal, she was able to lose herself in the careful needlework.

That was until there was a bump in the road and the carriage jerked suddenly to the left. Olivia's careful fingers slipped, and the needle jabbed into her finger.

"Ouch!" she exclaimed, instinctively raising the wounded finger to her mouth.

There was a cough. Olivia looked up to see Colin looking most uncomfortable as she stared with her finger in her mouth.

She removed it hastily and tried to think of something else. Embroidery was not going to do it, and as soon as her gaze left it, her memory returned to that kiss.

Her first-ever kiss. Even Harold had never done that.

"Is..." Colin swallowed before continuing. "Is your finger injured?"

"Only a needle prick," said Olivia quietly.

He nodded. "Good. I mean, not good, obviously, but I am glad it is nothing more serious. We can take a closer look at it when we stop. I am sorry to say that knowing the roads from London to Brighton now as we do, we cannot expect the roads for our journey to Bath to be any better. We will have to stop overnight, I think."

Olivia only managed, "Yes, I see."

How was it possible for her to disentangle herself now from this man who was overwhelming her senses?

"I do not mind," she added. "I am happy to stay another night on the road with you."

It was the wrong thing to say. A flush crept up the duke's neck, and he looked away.

Olivia looked down. She had bled a little on her embroidery, and it was ruined now.

At least it had kept her quiet, for who knew what would emerge from her mouth whenever she spoke! *She was happy to stay another night on the road with him?* The man would take it as a direct appeal for more kisses and more tender embraces!

Even if she did want them, even if her heart ached at the thought she would never again experience such things with him.

Olivia busied herself with putting the embroidery away carefully in her reticule. It was madness to think such things. Her first kiss, she had been firm on that with Harold. That was probably why Isabella...

No, she thought fiercely, pulling out a book, her only other refuge. She would not allow herself to be upset by the past. It was behind her, mostly, and Isabella had certainly never mentioned him again.

He mattered little to both Lymington twins, it turned out in the end. He was not worth her thoughts, not after what he had done, what Isabella had done to both of them.

"Interesting book?"

Olivia looked up. Colin had a bright smile on his face and was eager for conversation, but she could not allow herself that weakness.

"Yes," she said and then raised it a few inches so that it covered her eyes in a rather pathetic attempt to demonstrate that she was in no mood for conversation.

It did not, of course, prevent her from glancing at Colin once or twice in the next minute. He was no longer looking at her, but there was a disappointed look on his face.

Olivia tried not to feel pleased. She was supposed to be helping the man.

After all, the Lymingtons kept a house in Bath. It was the only place, reasonably, that Isabella could have gone. Within a day, all this would be over.

As the carriage meandered on, slowing at times to navigate its way through a tricky part of the road, Olivia found the pages of her book appeared to merge into one. Hadn't she already read this part? Even when she turned a few pages back and tried to take in the words printed on the page, none of them seemed to make sense.

"The news will get out eventually."

Olivia placed the bookmark back into her book and returned it to her lap. Colin was looking at her with a rueful expression.

"Everyone will know," he said quietly. "They will know she did not marry me."

Olivia's heart twisted. He looked so heart weary, and there was nothing she could do to counsel him or offer him words of comfort. *Except…*

Her gut balked at the idea, but in her heart, she knew it was the right thing to do. She could trust Colin. He would never betray her.

"Gossips always find these things out," Colin continued with a sigh, "and then it will be all over Town. I mean, look at what happened with the Devonshires! They got married in the end, and they say it was a love match, but of course, they would say that. They had to."

Olivia smiled. "I do not know the Devonshires well, but they do appear to…to be very much in love."

Colin shrugged. "So they say, but how are we to know? It could all be a cover to prevent a greater scandal, and I would not blame them."

"I have seen the way the duke looks at his wife," said Olivia with a wry smile. "I would say it was a love match."

He matched her smile, and Olivia felt her stomach drop. The way he looked at her…she was no expert, but it was not far from how the Duke of Devonshire looked at his wife.

What did it all mean? If only she was outspoken like Isabella or simply naïve like her two other sisters. Then she could have asked outright what the man meant by that or be completely oblivious to the fact.

Olivia could not hide from it, that she had now spent more time alone with the Duke of Larnwick than any other gentleman in the world!

"Still, I do not see how we, or your parents, can keep this out of the gossip pages," said Colin heavily. "I suppose I will simply have to accept it and return with Isabella to Scotland, never to return to Town again."

Olivia swallowed. This was the moment she must be honest, even if it would pain her.

"You…you would be surprised what you can keep quiet. With enough influence and enough gold."

She had expected Colin to be intrigued, but instead, he merely scoffed, his jaw tightening in that way that made her heart skip a beat.

"You do not believe me?" Olivia asked lightly. "You did not know I was engaged two years ago, did you?"

Now she had his attention. Colin's gaze snapped to her own as his mouth fell open. "You were?"

Olivia nodded. The carriage was warm, with blankets inside for long journeys, but she had never felt so warm as this.

"I had no idea," he said, leaning forward. "What happened? You're...you're not a widow, are you?"

His look of concern made Olivia laugh. "No, I am not a widow."

She had gone too far now to escape telling the whole story, but for some reason that Olivia did not quite understand, she did not mind. Colin Vaughn knowing her history would be a relief in a way.

"This was about...I don't know, six months before we met you," Olivia said quietly. "We met a gentleman called Harold Jones. He took a fancy to me. My parents liked him, and a match was made."

"You didn't love him?"

"No, but I did like him. There are precious few choices as a woman, Colin. Larnwick, I mean."

"I like Colin."

Olivia did not quite manage to hold his gaze. "I liked him. Or at least, I liked the attention he gave. I cannot tell now. It was all too long ago, too rushed. Anyway, two days before the wedding, he disappeared."

Colin's mouth fell open. "So you know, you understand the wild confusion of a missing betrothed?"

"Harold disappeared, and so did Isabella."

She did look at him now, though a little warily. *There, the truth about her, about Isabella.*

Colin had never looked so confused or astonished before. He had clearly lost the power of speech, attempting to say something several times before he coughed and then leaned back in his seat.

"So Isabella was married?"

It was not like Olivia to hesitate, but as the carriage rattled on, she knew she had to get this right. *To explain it poorly would be a disserve.*

"No, they never married," she said softly.

Colin's knees were touching her own now, he was leaning so close to her. "So you're telling me that they...that she is not..."

Olivia flushed. "I believe her to still be innocent if that's what you mean. They were found that evening at supper. But still. She took him from me. Even for my own wedding, I ended up being the second choice."

It was impossible to speak without bitterness. It was shameful to admit such a pathetic moment of her life, but at the same time, he needed to know. Isabella should have told him.

"See," she said softly. "No one ever found out. You did not even know I was engaged to be married. A great scandal, hidden carefully by the Lymington family."

And then she gasped. Colin had taken her hand, her gloves lying beside her on the seat. His skin burned hers, and as she looked up, his dark eyes looked deep within her own.

"Then he did not deserve you," Colin said softly.

Olivia nodded, unable to look away. Why was it that she had finally found her perfect gentleman, the only man who was likely to make her happy, only to find herself two years too late?

CHAPTER TEN

"GOOD EVENING, MISS Isabella. Oh, I see you are with your husband, so 'tis Your Grace now, I suppose!"

Colin sighed heavily. It was the third person to approach them with such a greeting in the inn where he and Olivia had decided to break their journey to Bath. None of them meant badly, he could see by their faces. Nay, they intended to be pleasant.

He watched Olivia's lips purse and then that smile he knew so well appear; controlled, restrained, definitely a smile but with absolutely no warmth.

"How kind of you to say," she said quietly.

"Oh, 'tis no trouble at all," said the lady with a knowing smile. "How many of us get to say that we have landed a duke?"

Olivia's gaze met Colin's, and he sighed heavily. *How was he supposed to make them stop?* Their meal, at least, was almost over. It would not be long before they could take their leave of the other diners, finally, and retreat upstairs.

"—never seen a duchess before, not in person," the lady chattered away. She had not seen fit to introduce herself, but Colin wondered whether that was on purpose. She must know how irritating she was being!

"How very kind," repeated Olivia in that quiet, unassuming tone. "But we must not keep you from your dinner, so I will bid you good evening."

The interloper blinked and looked at Colin. "Oh. Oh, I see. Good evening."

She stalked away rather haughtily, and Colin could not but smile at his companion.

"Very well done. Almost regal, far more impressive than a mere duchess."

Olivia rolled her eyes in that rather delightful way that was starting to make his heart beat faster. "It was very rude, I am afraid, but I could think of no other way around it. I simply wish to be left alone. Is that so difficult?"

Colin shook his head. "For some reason, the rank of duke does not encourage those of a lesser degree to stay away. It tires me. I would rather be in Scotland."

Where were these words coming from? He was not a gentleman to share his feelings, and Olivia was a woman he had known of for years but never really spoken with.

Until the last few days. Until they had stepped into a carriage together and found they had so much more in common than he ever had with his intended bride.

"You will be in Scotland soon," Olivia said lightly, pushing her plate away. "As soon as we find her, and that will be tomorrow, I am sure of it."

Colin smiled but did not say anything. *What could he say?* After another long day on the road, full of moments of temptation he should never have even noticed and opportunities for kisses that he managed not to take, what sort of a conversation could he have?

All he wanted was to be left alone with his thoughts.

Well, that was not entirely true. Colin watched Olivia as her gaze flickered around the room, examining the inn they were staying in this evening. He wanted to be alone with Olivia. No one else to interfere, to judge, to tell them that what he was feeling was wrong.

And it was wrong to feel this way, wasn't it? After all the waiting he had done for Isabella, all the other temptations he had avoided while anticipating their marriage, was he really about to cross this line?

Colin swallowed, and tried to finish the sort of stew served to them by a rather greasy landlord. It was sticky, stodgy food. The best you could find in an inn, and Colin had at first gulped it down, starving hungry after their decision not to stop for luncheon on the road.

Now it just tasted bland. He could not eat with these thoughts whirling round his head.

How could he explain what was occurring between them? Colin saw the pain that sparked in her eyes every time someone mistook her for her twin. He was the one who had put her in this position. He was the one who had decided to use her likeness as a way out for his shame, and each time he saw the anguish that it caused her.

He was selfish.

The way his body responded, the way he wanted to kiss her, to gently take that gown off her and touch her skin, know what it was like to bury himself inside her…

Colin coughed. *Dear God, if she knew what he wanted, what he was thinking!* If all had gone to plan, they already would be, yet here he was, wondering whether it would be possible to pretend there was only one room available!

Colin glanced at her. He had been worried at first that his penchant for silence would offend her, but Miss Olivia Lymington seemed perfectly happy to sit in companionable silence.

It was a rare gift. He could not recall ever encountering a young lady who was so…so well suited to him.

He wished to enjoy every moment he had with her. Even though these burgeoning feelings would have to be stripped away in the morning, once they had found her sister, it was pleasant to look at her and think, perhaps, that she really was his wife.

"I hope you do not mind that I enjoy silence," Olivia said, breaking it. "It is just…I have much on my mind."

Colin smiled. "I was just thinking the same thing. There are few people I can be so open with. It turns out that you are one of them."

And she smiled so prettily that Colin's stomach gave a painful lurch. *By God, was this…love?* Was he truly starting to have genuine affection for probably the one woman in the world he could not have?

Colin shifted uncomfortably in his seat, trying not to think about it all too much. Olivia had sacrificed so much for him already. Her own reputation was on the line if it was discovered the woman traveling with was not his wife.

"Is that…it is! The Duke of Larnwick!"

Colin blanched. He knew that voice, even though he had spent so little time in London. *Everyone knew that voice.*

"Lady Romeril!" Olivia said, wide-eyed. "How lovely to see you."

Colin turned slowly to see a sight he had not expected in an inn like this: Lady Romeril. She was past seventy years old, sharp as she had been fifty years ago, and kept most of society in line with a mixture of tongue lashings and gossip.

She was the last person they needed to meet on the road.

"Ah, Lady Romeril, what a shame you have come across us just as we are about to go up," said Colin hastily, rising and bowing low. "Such a shame."

"Indeed," said Lady Romeril. Her gaze left him and moved swiftly over to Olivia. "And this is the blushing bride, I take it."

It was not exactly a question, and Colin looked over at Olivia fearfully. The twins had undoubtedly met her several times. *Why, he had first met the Lymingtons at one of her balls!*

"Good evening, Lady Romeril," said Olivia quietly, bowing her head but not rising from her chair for a curtsey.

Colin forced down a smile. *Well, it was precisely what Isabella would do.* A newly made duchess would never deign to curtsey to a mere lady.

"Hmm," said the older woman, a frown appearing. "Not much changed since your marriage, I see. And yet…"

Colin saw Olivia flush before she said, "I am a married woman now, true, but I am sure I am much the same as I was."

"Then that would be a shame if you ask me," Lady Romeril said curtly. She never had been one to mince her words. "I take it you are off to Bath."

Olivia glanced instinctively at Colin, who nodded. "We are indeed, Lady Romeril. Will we have the pleasure of seeing you there?"

"I will be there, certainly, but whether you have the pleasure of my company is yet to be seen," said Lady Romeril with a stern expression. "I admit to being no great favorite of yours, Miss Isabella as you were, and I expect to see changes in you before you receive another invitation from me. Good evening."

The older woman stalked away.

"Well," said Olivia lightly as he dropped into his chair. "I am sorry I could not restore Isabella in her ladyship's good graces."

"I am sorry you had to put up with that," said Colin, but quietly in case, Lady Romeril heard him. She was a great one for listening across rooms. "Your last day as Isabella…"

He could not even finish the sentence. He could see the agony this encounter had caused.

This journey must have been torture for her, Colin mused. The sooner she could cast off the false guise of her sister, the better. Though if it had been up to him, the sooner she could cast off the clothes that hid that delectable beauty, the better…

"I think I will go up," said Olivia, rising. "I am tired."

Colin stood. "Yes, let me find out where our rooms are. I will only be a moment."

No matter what he said to the innkeeper, he could not convince the man to give them two rooms.

"Nay, I would not be the one to come between a man and his newly found wife," the innkeeper said comfortably. "I would not forgive myself if the two of you remained fighting for the sake of two rooms," said the innkeeper, a little more seriously. "Whatever has come between you, 'tis not right for a man and his wife to be so disagreeable. Why, I can see the affection between you from across the room! One room, Y'Grace, and I think you will thank me for it one day."

Colin was handed a key with a smile, and the innkeeper stepped away.

Heart thumping wildly, he stared at the key. *One key. One room. One bed.*

If he was honest, it was what he wanted, but it was wrong. She was forbidden from him as much as any woman, and this would not help the desire he was attempting to ignore.

Colin looked over at Olivia, who smiled across the room. His stomach lurched. *Ye gods, this was a disaster. He had fallen in love, not with his bride, but with her twin sister.*

There was nothing for it. He walked across the room, carefully sidestepping a pair of gentlemen who were happily telling each other how much they cared for each other, and stood before Olivia with a false smile upon his face.

"Let's away to our room."

"Our room?" Olivia was far sharper than he had given her credit for.

"Yes," he said helpless, "well, there was only one, so I…"

"Lady Romeril is watching. Kiss me."

Colin did not need much more of an invitation. He captured her lips in a passionate, deep kiss, and it was all he could do not to pull her into his arms.

There was a resounding cheer around the inn, and Colin broke the kiss. He had been so swept up in the moment, so eager to obey her instruction, he had not remembered they were standing in the middle of an inn with all and sundry watching them.

He glanced at Olivia, with flushed cheeks but a smile on her lips.

"Time to go upstairs," she whispered. Taking his hand, she led him to the staircase with more whoops and cheers.

Colin glanced over his shoulder just the once and saw to his satisfaction that Lady Romeril's cheeks were pink.

It was only when they had reached their bedchamber and shut the door behind them did Colin realize what they had just done. *It was scandalous!* They were playing with fire, and they both knew it.

Did she enjoy the drama of it all? The delight in teasing Lady Romeril?

Or, as Colin so desperately hoped, *was her fancy for him becoming something more?*

"I think I might get too accustomed to being Isabella at this rate," said Olivia quietly in a rueful voice. "I have been her now for what, four days?"

Colin swallowed. He was not entirely sure he had his breath back from that heady kiss. The room had a sofa, *thank God*. Olivia had sat on the end of the bed, and it would all be over if he joined her there.

"I hate that you are forced to mimic her," he said quietly, trying not to think of the sensation of her lips on his. "It will be over soon."

"'Tis important, though," she said lightly. "We have to protect your reputation."

Colin laughed as he pulled off his coat and threw it behind him on the armchair. "You seem to be far more interested in my reputation than your sister's or even your own, Olivia. What do you think will happen to you, to us, if it is found out who we actually are?"

Her hands tightened in a knot as she sat on the bed.

If found in a bedchamber with Miss Olivia Lymington, the two of them would not be unwed for long.

God's teeth, they were in for it now. This journey was supposed to be to find Isabella, not to fall in love with each other!

Twenty-four hours. That was all they had to manage, Colin thought desperately. As long as they did not do anything foolish, they would be safe.

"The important thing," said Olivia, as though she could read his thoughts, "is that tomorrow we should find her. I do not think she will leave Bath. She has nowhere else to go."

"A part of me hopes we won't find her."

Colin could hardly believe those words had come out of his mouth. *What had he been thinking?* He groaned, putting his head in his hands.

"Wh-What do you mean?"

He looked up and saw Olivia's expression; wonder, confusion, hope. *Damn.* They needed to be careful, but at the moment, he felt like throwing caution to the wind and just accepting the desire between them.

"I think you know," he said quietly. "You cannot have been ignorant of the feelings growing between us, Olivia. I find myself far more intrigued by you than your sister."

Olivia said nothing, but her eyes did not leave his own. A spark of hope leapt in Colin's heart, but it was quickly quashed.

"This feels all a fool's errand," he said quietly, finding his heart opening to her in a way it had never done before, not to anyone. "I am chasing after a woman I do not even know, when before me I have a woman who I respect, I like, who is so beautiful…"

This was a mistake, but he could not help himself. This would be the last day he and Olivia were alone, and he needed to speak this truth, even if he would regret it. Even if he did wed Isabella, he wanted Olivia to know. It was not she who was the second choice.

"You cannot think that way," Olivia whispered.

The distance between them was not much, a few feet. Colin wished he was closer, that he had been brave enough to sit on the bed with her.

If he had…

"You know I hardly knew Isabella when I offered marriage to her," Colin said wearily. "It cannot be a surprise to you. She seemed nice enough, and she was pretty…"

Olivia did not look shocked at his rather mercenary memory of their betrothal. "Remember, I have been your chaperone of a sort the last few years. I would have to be a fool to not see there was little love lost between you."

"I wish I had known you then."

Colin knew there was no taking these words back.

He swallowed. They had kissed twice now, but still, they had not crossed a line they could not come back from. But now, at this moment, despite promising himself that he would not, he was about to try to.

He wanted her. She wanted him. No one would know, and he could take precautions. There would be no consequences from such an act.

Besides, it did not feel wrong. *It felt right.* As though fate had intended them to be together, with the world around them convinced of their marriage.

Colin took a deep breath. "I know once this is said, it cannot be unsaid."

"Yes," said Olivia quietly. "But I think...I think I need to hear it."

It was the best encouragement he could hope for. "Look, she took someone from you, someone you cared about. I care about you far more than I believed possible. Olivia, would it not make you feel better to do the same thing, even for one night?"

"I have never sought revenge or retribution," said Olivia, but she did not look away. *She wanted him, Colin knew it.* "What do you want from me, Colin?"

Hearing his name on her lips pushed him over the edge. He would regret this, perhaps, but he would regret it far more if he did not offer himself to her.

Rising slowly from his seat, he stepped across the room and sat beside her. He lifted a hand gingerly and then with greater confidence. Olivia was looking at him with such desire he was surprised they were not already kissing.

Gently, Colin pushed a curl of hair behind Olivia's ear. She shivered at his touch, not moving away.

"Olivia," he said softly. "You are beautiful, and you deserve to know joy. I admit, these last few days, I have desired you more than I can say. More than I should say. Those kisses were perfect."

"We should not have done it."

"Yes, there are a lot of things I shouldn't do that I would like to do to you," said Colin quietly.

He watched Olivia swallow as his gaze moved down to her décolletage, her breasts, the way they heaved at the mere suggestion of lovemaking.

"You...you are talking madness."

"Look, I would never force you. We could take precautions, with no children made, just pleasure shared."

She said nothing but looked deep into his eyes.

"Besides I...I have affection for you," admitted Colin. *Damn, he had never been this vulnerable before!* Did she want him to beg on bended knee? "No one would ever have to know. This is our last night together, and I want you."

It was hard to tell whether he had gone too far or not far enough. The silence that hung between them was one he could not break, though he desperately wished to demand her answer.

No, this was not that kind of moment. She had to choose it, had to come to him willingly. Olivia's expression was so clouded, and he could not tell what she was thinking.

And then she nodded.

CHAPTER ELEVEN

OLIVIA SAT IN silence, fearful he would require her to speak her mind, and she was not entirely sure what the whirling thoughts were.

Except she wanted him.

Whatever it was that craved him, it was animalistic. This part of her, the Olivia that wished to throw caution to the wind and leap into his arms, was undoubtedly not the Olivia the world had seen in Almack's, at Lady Romeril's ball, or any card party of the Season.

No, this was a new part of her.

"No one would ever have to know. This is our last night together, and I want you."

How could she say no?

After the last few days, teasing and tantalizingly close yet never close enough, it was all Olivia could do not to kiss him now.

Was it a dream? Olivia resisted the impulse to pinch herself. This was certainly real; she could feel the weight of him beside her, the thin mattress on the bed leaning toward her. She could feel his gaze on her skin as Colin looked at her body, blatantly desiring to touch her.

And she wanted him to.

If she could have him for a night…

Just a night.

Her body craved him. *Who was she to deny herself?*

It not as though anyone would ever know. As far as the world knew, she was Isabella Vaughn, Duchess of Larnwick. It was only natural she and her husband would make love, though it was something a little more fiery that she had in mind.

But are you just the second choice here?

"I want you to be sure," said Colin quietly. "I have no wish for you to feel pressured into this. God, I want you, but you have to choose it freely. Freely, Olivia."

Olivia tried to think. He was everything she wanted, and though she knew this night would not change their fates, it would give her a moment to remember.

"I choose you freely, Colin."

Olivia knew she was certain. She could not regret this, not truly.

"Olivia," Colin breathed.

His lips worshipped her own, his tongue gently teasing until she allowed him entrance, and Olivia knew that it was in this moment that she was coming alive for the first time.

How could she have lived a life without these sensations? Though it was only her mouth that he was kissing, every inch of her body was vibrating with the pleasure that only Colin knew how to spark within her.

She had spent her life asleep, and only now was she awakening to the possibilities.

It did not seem real, and yet in the whole world, there was nothing more natural than Colin Vaughn, the Duke of Larnwick, who was kissing her as though without her, he would crumble. She was all that seemed to be supporting him, and Olivia was glad, privileged to be sharing this moment with him.

"Oh, Olivia," Colin murmured, finally breaking the kiss they shared but only to tease more kisses down her neck.

She shivered.

There must have been something in her body that shifted, for Colin immediately withdrew his hands and pushed himself back on the bed.

"Are you well?" he asked urgently, his eyes seeking out her gaze. "Am I going too fast? Would you like me to slow down, to stop?"

Olivia shook her head. There did not appear to be words for how she was feeling, and though she wanted him desperately, there was hesitancy.

There was something holding her back, and though she had the words to ask, Olivia was a little embarrassed to spell it out so clearly.

But she had to. *This could not continue unless she understood.*

"You...you said," she started. "About...you said that there would be no consequences, no...no child. I do not understand."

Colin's face, a picture of confusion, immediately relaxed. "Ah, that is simple."

He moved from the bed, stepping away and causing a wrench in Olivia's heart. She wanted Colin close to her, as close as could be.

"Here," said Colin.

He was holding out something he had retrieved from his trunk. It was an envelope, and within it, a strange sort of thing that Olivia had never seen before.

"What is it?"

"A preservative," said Colin matter-of-factly, seating himself by her once more. "They are from France typically. A gentleman wears it over his manhood and prevents a child from being created."

Olivia could feel her cheeks burning, but she nodded as she looked down at the strange item. Enjoy pleasure without any consequences.

A life of hedonism without repercussions.

"You understand?"

Olivia nodded.

"Colin," she said, reaching for him. "I want you."

She had to feel him, really feel him. She wanted the sensation of his skin against hers. All these clothes, they were getting in the way.

"Woah there," said Colin gently, breaking the kiss between them and capturing her fingers in his own. "Come here."

There was no harshness in his words, and Olivia obeyed immediately, rising from the bed and standing beside it opposite him.

"Now," said Colin, smiling encouragingly, "undress me."

Olivia blinked. "Wh-What? I thought you wanted me to stop?"

Colin closed the gap between them, took her face in his hands, and kissed her slowly. This was a different kiss; passionate, yes, but more than that. Devotional. Reverent.

"Yes, I did," he said eventually in a low voice and with a wry smile. "But only as you would find it easier like this. Take off my clothes."

She wanted to rip his clothes from his body, see whether the delectable duke was just as delicious underneath all his garb.

But she couldn't just strip him. It would never do to lose control.

Colin smiled encouragingly, his eyes full of desire. Olivia swallowed. And once she had removed his clothes…he would remove hers.

Slowly, her fingers no longer fumbling, moved to the buttons on his waistcoat. It was difficult, standing this close and not kissing him, and Olivia saw no reason to restrict herself.

Lifting her lips to his, Olivia closed her eyes and reveled in the pleasure his tongue gave her as her fingers slowly moved down his waistcoat. Then the last button was undone, and she did not break the kiss as she gently pulled it over his shoulders and allowed it to drop to the floor.

It was Colin who broke the kiss as he groaned, "God's teeth, Olivia, but you're making me wild for you!"

She could feel her breathing quicken as the buttons of his shirt slowly became undone under her quick fingers, and she gasped as she pulled it from his body and allowed it to fall to the floor.

He was beautiful.

"Oh, Colin," she breathed.

It took but a moment for her to undo his breeches, and he removed his boots and the rest of his clothing to stand before her, utterly naked.

Olivia could not help it. Her eyes were drawn, inextricably, to that part of him which she knew was to form such an essential part of their evening. His manhood. She wanted to touch it, wanted to know what it felt to have such a thing in her hand.

"When you look at me like that, God alive…"

Olivia smiled. It was intoxicating, having this sort of power over him. Now he could start to understand how she felt when she looked at him.

"May I undress you?"

Olivia nodded and was unsurprised to find that Colin knew his way around a gown. In less than a minute, her gown had pooled to the floor along with her corset, releasing her breasts in a swift movement and then her undershift.

She was naked. She had expected to feel self-conscious, to feel a desire to hide and keep his gaze away.

But she didn't. She was offering herself to Colin with nothing held back. All she wanted now was…

"Come here," Colin said in a rough voice.

How long they stood there in each other's arms, Olivia could not tell. She had no memory of falling onto the bed as they found new ways to make each other gasp with their kisses.

"I want…" she gasped, utterly unable to describe what she wanted but knowing he could give it to her. "I want more, Colin. I want you, I want…"

"I know," he said with a jagged voice. "I know. You have to trust me, Olivia. I need to warm you up first."

Olivia could not comprehend what he could mean. She had never felt more warm in her life, her very soul on fire, but then his fingers gently made their way to her secret place, and she suddenly understood there was much she had to learn.

"Oh, Colin!"

She clung to him as the pleasure built within her, not knowing precisely where it was going but feeling the peak rising. *There was such ecstasy in the world!*

"Yes, yes, yes!"

Her entire body shuddered with pleasure as something exploded within her. Once she opened her eyes, she saw Colin biting his lip.

"What is wrong?"

"Wrong?" gasped Colin with a laugh. "I almost came seeing you! Are…are you ready for me?"

Olivia nodded. "Yes. Yes, love me, Colin."

Here they were, at the point of no return, and there was not a doubt in her mind. He was her fate. This was all meant to be, and after quickly putting on the preservative and entering her slowly, Olivia knew she loved him more than she would ever love another person.

"Olivia, you feel so…" breathed Colin, seemingly unable to finish his sentence. "Oh, hell!"

What happened next was instinct.

And as Colin built the rhythm, his pace increasing slowly as Olivia arched her back with the pleasure, she knew this was it. She would never share this with another man. She never could.

"Colin!" she cried out as he brought her to pleasure again. "Yes!"

When he finally plunged into her and cried out, it was, "Olivia, Olivia, yes!"

Hearing her name on his lips as he poured himself into her pushed her over the edge once more. He was everything, they were everything, and they clung to each other as Colin collapsed into her arms.

She kissed his neck. "Thank you."

Colin turned his head and smiled. "I think I should be the one thanking you."

He kissed her deeply before pulling her into his arms.

"I…I hope we did not disturb anyone," murmured Olivia. Now the fire of passion was over, it was a rather strange thought to think another person could have heard her lose her innocence.

She felt Colin chuckle as well as heard him. “I hope we did.”

Olivia laughed. This was it. This was everything. As she fell asleep in his arms, she knew she would never be this happy again.

CHAPTER TWELVE

OLIVIA LYMINGTON.

She was beautiful. Every inch of her was far more impressive than he had imagined, and now he had touched her all over, his fingertips cried out to do so again.

He had bedded her, and though he could hardly believe they had been so bold with their desires, he found there was not a single regret in his heart.

What they had done was right. There was no guilt, no feelings he should have held back. What he and Olivia had shared was perfect. It had been like poetry.

As though Fate had placed them here and smiled down on them as they shared something so precious and wonderful that there was no one alive who could deny them.

Colin swallowed as the warm feelings faded and the reality of the situation crept in.

He had not meant this to happen.

Today was the day they entered Bath and found Isabella. He would step away from Olivia, the woman he knew meant more to him than any other, and instead take to his side a woman who looked very like her, but in every meaningful way was a world apart.

How would he do it?

Colin's jaw tightened. *He would do his duty.* So would Isabella. They would do what they had to do because they had to. *They would make heirs, but they wouldn't make love.*

Olivia shifted in her sleep, murmuring something Colin could not make out. His heart twisted as he looked at her, warm and trusting. In her dreams, they could be together. Even as he had to face the awful truth that today would tear them apart.

How could he have ever looked at the Lymington twins and considered them the same! Colin felt a fool now for even thinking it, let alone voicing it to Olivia just days ago.

They were so different, and it was a wonder that they came from the same parents, let alone were twins.

Colin sighed slowly, trying not to wake Olivia. The longer he looked at her, seeing her beauty, remembering her kindness, recalling the hedonistic pleasure they had shared...

It was a wonder he was still going after Isabella.

Tomorrow, probably, he would make Isabella his wife.

"Those look like deep thoughts, Colin."

He jerked. His contemplations had so overtaken his attention; he had not even noticed Olivia had awoken with a wry smile.

"They are indeed," he murmured with a smile of his own. "Good morning, Olivia."

Olivia snuggled closer to him. "Good morning."

Only then did the realization of the situation, that they were naked together in bed, come into his mind. She must have read his thoughts, for she looked suddenly worried.

"What will happen when everyone finds out?" Olivia whispered. "Colin, Lady Romeril is in this inn!"

That was certainly a sobering thought, and Colin found himself pulling the covers up around him at the very idea of Lady Romeril discovering them.

"Oh, what have I done?" She looked devastated, as if she regretted everything.

Colin's jaw tightened. *He should have predicted this.* Though it hurt him beyond measure to see her pain and regret, what could he do?

Young ladies simply did not do this sort of thing. Allowing a gentleman to kiss you without simultaneously offering marriage was enough to get a lady into trouble. And this?

No wonder she was so afraid of what would happen if they were discovered.

Colin tried to remember all this as he looked at Olivia.

"Please, do not upset yourself, Miss Lymington," he said stiffly, wishing to protect both of them.

Olivia looked up hastily. "Miss Lymington?"

Colin shrugged with a touch of exasperation. "Well, it is quite clear that you wish us to pretend that nothing has happened! I am hardly likely to tell anyone, and you are not either. There is no chance anyone would find out."

But Olivia did not seem likely to believe him. "People will know! We have stayed here as husband and wife, and it is not impossible that someone…someone heard us."

Colin swallowed.

"If people do think that," he said slowly, "they will not know you are…you. They will think you are Isabella."

"I can…I can hardly believe it."

Colin smiled. There she was, the woman he had fallen in…the woman he had bedded. "I could not believe so much pleasure was to be had. You had some, too?"

"Oh, yes," Olivia said and then raised a hand to her mouth in shock at what she had said. "I mean…this is all so confusing, Colin. I never thought I would give up my innocence."

"You would be surprised," said Colin without thinking.

Olivia frowned. "Would I? How many ladies have you bedded?" She eased out of bed and crossed the room to get her clothes.

"All this conversation, when we should think about getting moving!" said Colin hastily. *That was not a topic he wished to dwell on.* "Now, Olivia. I tell you again, and please do not concern yourself with what the world will think. The world knows nothing."

Olivia nodded but did not speak, and Colin found his heart contracting painfully. He would do almost anything for her, and if he could take away all this strain that pretending to be her sister was putting on her, he would.

Today was the last day she would ever have to answer to the name Isabella.

"Can we…can we just forget that this ever happened?"

Colin stiffened. Olivia was looking at him from across the room in a most beseeching way, and it could not be more clear she wished for the events of last evening to be wiped out.

Christ, what could he say? There was a war ongoing in his heart.

But he would do what she asked. *He would do anything she asked at this moment.*

"I would never do or say anything you were uncomfortable with," he said gently. "Ask for my silence, and I will not only never speak of it to anyone, but I will never raise the topic with you, either. If that is what you want."

There was a small part of him that hoped she would refuse the second offering. That it was as special to her as it was him. *That she would wish to relive the moment when they…*

"Thank you," Olivia said quickly, a look of relief on her face. "Yes, that is a good idea. Thank you, Your Grace."

Your Grace. Colin almost closed his eyes in pain at the formality. Was this how easily they slipped back into the painful stiffness of formal language?

After all they had shared, this was all it came down to?

He nodded. He owed that to her after promising so much. "Right then. Well. We will not speak of it."

It was only a few minutes before they were dressed and ready to go. God, the sooner he could return to his valet, the better.

The two trunks were heavy in his arms as Colin started down the staircase, but they grounded him, gave him something to focus on other than the pain in his chest.

Miss Lymington was right. They had to act as though none of this had happened.

"Ready?" he said gruffly to her.

Olivia nodded, but before they could leave, they were accosted by the innkeeper.

"Ah, Your Graces! A pleasant evening and good sleep?" There was a rather knowing look on his face, and Colin saw to his dismay that Olivia blushed furiously.

"Do not worry, Your Grace," said the innkeeper with a wink. "Every newlywed bride is allowed to blush!"

These words only made Olivia blush all the more, and Colin could not help but feel sorry for her as he saw the pain on her face.

This was all his fault. He had accepted her offer of attending the journey to find Isabella, and it had been his wild idea that she should impersonate her sister when required.

He had to distract the innkeeper before Olivia melted onto the floor with embarrassment!

"How far are we from Bath, sir?" he asked.

The innkeeper thankfully turned his attention away from Olivia. "Ah, I would say only about five miles."

Colin glanced at Olivia. They had spent far too much time in that carriage, and it would be dangerous indeed for them to be alone in it today. Not after they had already succumbed to the passions deep below the surface.

"Are you up for a ride, something a little different from a carriage?" he asked quietly.

Olivia seemed to understand. "Yes, a ride. A ride would be most pleasant."

Her gaze quickly dropped to the floor. Colin did not attempt to meet it. He knew better than to push her when she felt so vulnerable.

"A ride! What a wonderful idea, and I just so happen to have two fine horses for the hiring," said the innkeeper, clearly spotting a chance to make a little more money. "And I can easily send your luggage by the next mail coach, to…?"

He looked expectantly at them, and Colin found himself looking at Olivia for an address. *He had barely ever been to Bath, after all.*

"To the Old Bell Hotel," she said quietly. "They always have rooms."

The two horses brought round were good, even he had to admit. He held out his hand to Olivia beside the mounting block, but she did not take it, mounting without assistance.

Colin assumed she was accustomed to riding, but she was holding herself so stiffly, he wondered whether she had an aversion to horses. Only when he mounted, and they started along the Bath road did he realize. *How could he expect her to sit comfortably when just hours before, he had taken her virginity?*

He needed to make conversation. As their horses trotted along the road, clearly eager for the exercise, Colin cleared this throat. "How is your horse?"

"Perfectly fine," came the stilted answer. It did not encourage a response.

Colin sighed. "I hope you do not mind forgoing the carriage. I thought a little fresh air—"

"Very pleasant."

But Colin was not going to merely give in. They had shared something, and even if she wanted to forget it entirely, he could not. He would not speak of it, but that did not mean it had not happened.

"What will you do?" he asked quietly as the road curved around a corner. "When we find her?"

"I am not sure. I suppose I will return to London," she said quietly. "To my parents."

It all felt wrong.

"And you?"

Colin sighed. "Go back to Scotland, I suppose. The rolling hills, the brooks, the lochs."

"I would like to visit one day," said Olivia wistfully. She allowed her mare to get a little closer to his stallion. "It sounds so beautiful."

"I am sure you will, when..." Colin almost stopped himself from saying it, but he ploughed on. *They could no longer pretend.* "When you visit your sister."

That was sufficient to end the conversation. They rode in silence, Colin wondering whether he could have done anything differently and realizing that it was years ago when he should have done something to change his fate.

He had proposed to Isabella and had his fun with Olivia. But it had to end there. *Tomorrow he would be married, and to the right twin.*

CHAPTER THIRTEEN

"WOAH THERE," OLIVIA murmured to the mare that she had become fond of over the last few hours.

There were few horses that would accept a new mistress so willingly for a ride like this.

Far more obliging than her own heart. It had torn in half just hours ago when she had realized the seriousness of her actions. It was madness, yet she had reveled in it.

Reveled in him.

Olivia glanced at the gentleman riding alongside her and quickly looked away. She would not tempt herself nor cause herself any further grief. It was enough that she had been forced to exact a promise from him that she knew he had not wished to make.

If only he had known how unwillingly she had asked him to make it. Olivia's heart panged at the thought of never revisiting their passion, but she could not think of herself.

She had to think of him.

If they were fortunate, and they found Isabella this evening as expected, then tomorrow they would be married. It was her duty as someone who loved him to free Colin from the potential harm her presence could inflict on him.

"There we are."

She looked up. Colin had spoken quietly, so softly she had almost missed it. There it was, Bath. The last of the afternoon sun was beaming down onto the white buildings, making them glow a beautiful orange, but she could not see the beauty.

How could she, when her heart was breaking?

She had done what she had told herself not to do. She had fallen in love with her sister's betrothed!

She should never have agreed to come on this journey. She should have known that spending days in his company would lead to one thing only.

"I have never come into Bath this way," he said from beside her. "'Tis pretty."

Olivia nodded, not able to trust her voice. After a day of riding, they had done it. They had reached Bath, where Isabella was certain to be found.

What would she do without him? How could any other man compare?

"We should continue on," Olivia found herself saying to break the silence. "We are losing the light. We should be in town before dark if we want to see Isabella this evening."

Without waiting for a reply, she nudged her mare on. Colin followed suit, his stallion's longer stride meaning he caught up with her quickly.

"Yes, we could go and see her this evening," he said quietly. "Or…or tomorrow."

Olivia's breath caught in her throat. "I beg your pardon?"

"Just a thought," said Colin hastily. "With clear heads, I was thinking, after a good night's sleep. That sort of thing."

He had not looked at her for a single syllable of that speech, and do what she could, Olivia could not prevent her heart from soaring.

Why was he suggesting another evening together before they found Isabella? *Did he wish to spend one more night with her?*

"Perhaps," she said as noncommittally as she could manage. "Let us get into town and see."

She would have to be strong. Olivia was not sure whether she had it in her, but she had to try. Another evening in Colin's arms would only make separation even more painful.

The town of Bath was not large, though it was busy. The Season had begun in earnest, and there were carriages all over the place. Colin and Olivia were forced to wait a few minutes at one road where they needed to cross, and Olivia felt her cheeks start to burn.

If she had been worried about being spotted and talked about in the inn last night, where there had only been perhaps twenty people at the most, what would happen here?

There would be much gossip around the two of them: newlyweds, a duke and duchess…how would she avoid their looks? How would they find a church that would marry them when the whole world believed her already married to the duke?

"Good day, Miss Isabella. No, I see it is Your Grace now!"

A gentleman Olivia hardly recognized inclined his head from his horse as he passed them. She barely had enough time to return the courtesy before he was gone.

"Ah, the Duke and Duchess of Larnwick!" came the cry from a person on the pavement as they passed them. "You are finally in town!"

Olivia did not know them, and Colin made no move to slow down and stop, so she did not either. It was remarkable how many people greeted her as her sister, and it was only after the fifth person did so that she realized what that meant.

"You are finally in town!"

If they had seen Isabella, the real Isabella, then they would not be so surprised she was finally in town, as one person had put it. *Isabella must be keeping a low profile.* Well, that was something she had never done. Perhaps it would be good for her to disappear into the corners of society.

But why?

"Here we are," she said aloud, a little self-conscious after not speaking for so long. "The Old Bell Hotel."

Colin nodded. "Excellent. Let's go in and secure a r…secure lodgings."

Olivia swallowed. He had been close to saying a room; she knew it. Were they ever to escape what they had shared?

"Here, let me help you."

Colin was reaching out to help her down from the horse, with no mounting block to descend.

If only she was a better horsewoman. Her youngest sister could jump down from any horse with no fear, but that was not a skill Olivia had ever garnered.

There was nothing for it. She took the proffered hand and jumped as lightly as she could down to the pavement. Colin's strong arms caught her, and Olivia found herself lingering a little too long.

Who could blame her? As she looked up, feeling the hurried beating of his heart through his greatcoat, Olivia wondered what would happen if they cast caution to the wind.

Neither of them was married, and she had no prior attachments to disrupt their happiness.

Colin's eyes were dark, darker than she had ever seen before. *If she allowed herself to remain here just a little longer, perhaps he would…*

Olivia stepped back. "I think most of Bath is surprised to see us here."

She hoped he would understand her meaning, and he nodded. "I would say she is either hiding or continuing under your name."

Olivia had not considered this as the footmen bowed low to Colin as he instructed them on the horses. *Isabella here in Bath, living under her name, and Olivia now here in the same town, pretending to be her sister.*

Would it not just be easier if they could continue like this? These were the lives they could not have expected, after all, and yet they seemed to be thriving.

She was, at any rate. Isabella had chosen to run, and Olivia was much happier living under Isabella's name. She could stay with Colin and…

No. Olivia took another step away and tried to calm her frantic thoughts. *No, she had played second fiddle to Isabella all her life.*

"Ah, Your Graces."

Olivia turned to see what could only be the hotel manager.

"A certain innkeeper sent word on the mail coach you would be staying here," he said. "I have prepared your room."

Olivia's heart sank. *No, not again. Not after all they had been through.* "Room?"

The hotel manager looked between them. "Is there a problem?"

She looked at Colin, trying to convey without words just how desperately she needed her own room.

"The thing is," said Colin delicately, taking a step closer to the hotel manager as he kept his voice low, "is that we had hoped for two rooms. Two separate rooms."

Olivia flushed. It was bad enough being forced to pretend to be Colin's wife, but now they were giving the impression they had already fallen out less than a week from the wedding.

However, she should not have worried. Instead of looking scandalized, the hotel manager winked. "Trouble in paradise?"

Olivia glared and then looked fiercely at Colin, who in turn glared at the hotel manager with such a regal gaze, she was sure even Lady Romeril would have been impressed.

"Ah," said the hotel manager with a discomforted look, straightening his waistcoat. "Unfortunately, Your Grace, I have but the—"

"One room," they chorused.

Olivia could not believe it. *What were the chances?* Though now she came to think about it, her gaze flickering across the numerous people teeming along the pavement, she should not have been surprised.

This was Bath at the beginning of the Season. It felt inevitable that of all the hotels she could have chosen, there would, of course, be only one room.

Olivia sighed. It seemed to be her lot in life, pretending to be her sister in increasingly upsetting circumstances. *At least tonight would be the last?*

"Fine," said Colin wearily but giving the hotel manager a dark look. "I suppose if that is the best you can do."

The man bowed low and scuttled back into the hotel, muttering about the best possible linens and a complimentary bottle of wine.

"What a long ride," she said. *Anything to fill the silence.* "I think we should—"

"Eat? Yes, so do I," interrupted Colin with a smile. "Your sister will have to be found tomorrow, I think. The night is drawing in."

Olivia looked around. He was right; the sun had disappeared, and she had barely noticed it.

"I think this hotel has a restaurant," said Colin, taking a step toward it. "Let us dine."

Olivia nodded and followed him without another word. How could she argue against his logic? She certainly was starving; they had had no luncheon on the road, a mistake in hindsight, and had a strange feeling she could not entirely ignore that Colin preferred to be around other people rather than be alone.

The hotel was bustling, and she expected to be turned away from the restaurant, but as a footman rushed toward them, Olivia saw with a wry smile that the hotel manager was looking over at them nervously.

It appeared they were about to receive the best service of their lives.

As they walked toward the table that had been hastily prepared for them, Olivia noticed the Marnions and the Coulsons were also there. It was only a matter of time before they were recognized.

"How delightful," she said pointedly, "that so many *friends of my parents* are here."

Colin glanced to where she was looking. "Do you think we should eat in the room?"

Olivia considered his suggestion. It would undoubtedly reduce the risk of gossip, but then she would have to sit with him in the room all alone, and she was not entirely sure that she trusted herself.

She took a deep breath. "No, let's eat here. We have nothing to hide."

"Other than ourselves," said Larnwick with a wry smile as two footmen pulled out chairs for them.

Olivia flushed, and by the time she had gotten a hold of herself, Colin had already ordered food.

"So," said Colin. "You will be returning to London."

"Yes," she replied quietly.

They fell into silence as they waited for their food. *Did she want him to ask her to stay?* To be a chaperone for Isabella until they were married, or longer, to live with them?

Olivia knew that there were such arrangements made by sisters, though often it was to ensure the unmarried one would meet plenty of her brother-in-law's friends.

How could she live with Colin and Isabella? *Her jealousy, hardly under control as it was, would entirely spiral!*

"Yes, back to London," Olivia repeated. "And you…you will go back to Scotland."

"Yes, eventually."

Olivia risked another question. "And what then?"

"Then?" He frowned. "What do you mean, then?"

"Well, you know, the rest of your life," said Olivia a little awkwardly. "What will you do? What did you do as a duke before you came down to London—"

"To marry Isabella," said Colin, finishing her sentence.

She nodded. *It was not a name she wished to speak, not now. Not after…*

Colin sighed heavily, picking up a fork and playing with it. "Do what most dukes do, I suppose. Have lots of children."

Olivia smiled as the buzz of the restaurant rose in volume, hiding their conversation from those around them. "I can certainly see you as the doting father."

"Strangely, so can I," said Colin ruefully. "It's something I have always wondered about, how many children I will have, but I would like at least four."

"Four! I can tell you from experience, having four children is no small thing," laughed Olivia, feeling for the first time in hours that they were back to how they had been. "I think I would like a few, too, starting with a boy called—"

"Thomas."

They had both spoken simultaneously. Olivia laughed, looking down at her lap, unable to hold his gaze. How was it possible that they were so perfect for each other?

He was everything she wanted. While she could sit for a while and pretend that this was her life, just visiting Bath, it was not to be. *Not for much longer.*

"Your food, Your Graces."

Olivia jumped. She had not noticed the footmen approaching, but her stomach stirred as they placed before her the most incredible concoction of salmon and vegetables.

Colin nodded his head dismissively, and the footmen melted away. He reached for her hand.

Olivia almost gasped at the sensation. *Not only was his hand warm and making hers tingle, but they were in public!*

"We shouldn't," she whispered. "Not here."

Not ever was what she should have said, but she could not help herself.

"Do not concern yourself," Colin whispered in return. "Everyone thinks we are newlyweds. They would never guess otherwise."

"My God, is that Larnwick? It is, as I live and breathe!"

Olivia snatched her hand away from Colin as a gentleman she recognized but could not immediately name approached their table with a laugh.

"Jacob Beauvale, what the devil are you doing here?" Colin had risen to his feet with a grin and clapped the gentleman on the back. "And the wife, she is here, too?"

"Just as yours is, good evening, Your Grace, and you must forgive my discourtesy! If I did not know your husband so well, I would never consider it," said Mr. Beauvale with a charming grin.

Olivia nodded, her heart twisting painfully. It could not be more obvious that Colin's friend believed her to be Isabella, and though she hated it, there was little she could do.

"Ah, then you must join us for dinner!"

Olivia stared at Colin. *What did he think he was doing, inviting these two strangers, for that was what they were to her, to their table?* How was she to pretend to be Isabella for hours with these people?

"Oh, we simply couldn't," said Mr. Beauvale.

"Nonsense, I insist," Colin said with feeling. "Isabella and I do not mind, do we, Isabella?"

Olivia hesitated before replying. "Of course not. Do join us, Mr. Beauvale."

She reserved her glare for when the man turned around to beckon his wife over.

How dare Colin do this to her! How could he call her Isabella so easily? Had he forgotten so quickly that she was a different woman?

But she had to keep her emotions under control. It was just one more day. A few more hours of agony...and then the real pain would start.

Chapter Fourteen

"Here, take my light."

Colin leaned forward gratefully as Jacob offered his tinderbox. He had been without a cigar for over a day now, and though he had never considered himself desperate, it was impressive how quickly his nerves were calmed as the smoke was inhaled into his lungs.

Not that it could do much good. Not with Olivia beside him, forced to pretend for the last two hours that she was her sister.

Colin breathed out slowly. *Well, there had been nothing else for it, worse luck.* As soon as he had seen Jacob approach their table, he knew they would suffer another pretense.

"Goodness, I had no idea how late the hour was!" Mrs. Beauvale yawned. She was a pretty woman, absolutely devoted to her husband. *Her second husband, from memory.* "I admit myself exhausted. Jacob, I think I will go up and check on the children."

Jacob chuckled good-naturedly. "What you mean is, you will go up and check on the children and immediately collapse into bed!"

His wife's eye twinkled as she replied, "When you give birth to children, my dear, then and only then may you lecture me about it."

She kissed him on the top of his head, and Colin could not help but watch, fascinated. It was not as though his parents' marriage had been bad, exactly. No, in the best fashion of the time, it had been arranged.

They had been perfectly cordial to each other whenever Colin had seen them, and his father had appeared to genuinely grieve for his mother when she had died unexpectedly.

But this…

Jacob and Elizabeth loved each other. There was passion there, as well as care. They laughed together, no frantic bitter sniping he had witnessed between other couples.

Elizabeth turned to them. "Your Graces, it was very pleasant to dine with you this evening."

"The pleasure is all ours," began Colin, but Olivia's actions superseded his words.

She rose from the table. "I think I will retire also."

Colin blinked. He had not expected to be separated so quickly. "Now?"

Olivia nodded, though she did not quite meet his eyes. "Yes, it has been a long day, and Mrs. Beauvale is right. The hour is late."

Only then did her gaze meet his. Colin almost smiled but managed to control himself. It was not merely the ride that had exhausted her if he was any judge.

No, it was being kept up late last night with their passion.

It was a bittersweet reminder of what had been.

"What a shame to be devoid of your company, Your Grace," said Jacob to Olivia with a smile. "I admit, I have greatly enjoyed our conversation. I wish you a good night's sleep."

He inclined his head, and Olivia curtseyed low.

"Where is your room," Mrs. Beauvale started saying as the two ladies walked away. "Ah, close to ours then! When was the last time you were in Bath? Oh, I used to live here, you know…"

Colin watched the two ladies walk away appreciatively. There was something rather delicious about the way Olivia's bottom curved in that gown. One had to be paying attention due to the way the fabric fell, but it was a heady reminder of the time both his hands had been clasped on…

No. No, that would not help anyone, least of all himself. She was beautiful, yes, but she was Olivia. She was supposed to be Isabella!

It was Jacob's laughter that brought him back to his senses. Colin looked across the table and saw the younger man chuckling as he tapped his cigar ashes onto the ornament provided by the hotel.

"What?" said Colin a little too defensively as he came to think about it.

"My dear man, you have it bad!"

Colin blinked, his stomach turning over. "What do you mean?"

"My dear Larnwick, are you trying to tell me that you don't know?"

It was all Colin could do to stay calm. There was no possibility Jacob could have worked it out, could he? Was it possible he had noticed a difference? Had worked out, perhaps, that this was not Isabella after all?

The restaurant in the hotel was almost empty now, the hour being so late, and the only other people in it were on the other side of the room. There was no chance they could overhear this conversation, was there?

"'Tis nothing to be ashamed of, man," said Jacob genially, taking another draw on his cigar. "Why, it could not be clearer."

"What could not be clearer?" asked Colin, trying to keep his voice level.

If it was necessary to hide the truth from Jacob, what could he do? Money? The man was wealthy enough from what the scandal sheets had mentioned—applying to his character, perhaps? Begging him not to…

"You have fallen in love with her!" crowed Jacob.

Colin waited for the rest of the statement, but that was it.

"Finally, after so long!" Jacob added. "I mean, I saw the two of you in London, in Bath, too. Not sure who I felt more sorry for, to tell the truth."

Colin stiffened. *So Jacob had not realized the twins had swapped places?*

"Really?" he said, suddenly aware that he had a responsibility to keep the conversation going.

Jacob nodded. "I know not all matches are made from love and affection, but there is usually some sort of desire there, and yet whenever I saw you look at Isabella before you wed, I saw naught but patience there. And now, look at you!"

Colin swallowed. "I don't know what you're talking about."

Jacob was jesting with him, wasn't he?

Jacob sighed. "It is so strange, isn't it?"

"What?" asked Colin, attempting to keep up.

"Love," mused his companion. "Some husbands do not fall in love with their wives until months or even years after the wedding. Whereas I fell in love almost a year before she even agreed to marry me!"

Colin laughed, relieved somewhat that the conversation had moved away from himself and Olivia. "Yes, but in all fairness, Beauvale, she was a widow with her late husband's child on the way. She had much to think of, none of which was you."

Was it his imagination, or did Jacob's gaze drop a little there, refusing to meet his?

He had heard the rumors. He may have been journeying down from Scotland at the time, but a potential scandal of that sort was large enough to reach him on the road.

The Right Honorable Elmore Howard had died in mysterious circumstances, were the whispers, and his widow, Mrs. Elizabeth Howard, was suddenly with child. It was a miracle after years of barren marriage.

And a certain Jacob Beauvale was calling rather often…

"Yes," said Jacob slowly. "Yes, it was rather sudden."

"Rather dramatic, from what I heard," said Colin, trying not to tease but unable to resist.

His friend nodded. "Yes, well. It was all rather complicated."

Colin waited, but Jacob did not seem in the mood to share any further. His curiosity was piqued now, and he had a desire to know the full tale. It could not be too scandalous, after all. Here they were, married and with a child of their own to add to the child Elizabeth had already borne before they were wed.

"Complicated sounds interesting, and I could do with some entertainment," said Colin.

It must have been a trick of the light or the tiredness of Colin's own eyes. For a moment, Jacob's face seemed overcast by a shadow.

"Well, there is not much to tell," he said awkwardly, eyes downcast. "I was engaged to another woman at the time that Elizabeth and I…well, you may as well know, it was in all the gossip. I'm surprised you had not already heard. I can barely believe I did it myself."

"Did it?" prodded Colin curiously. "Did what?"

Jacob took a deep breath and smiled deprecatingly. "I am a cad, Your Grace. I actually ran out of that wedding to marry Elizabeth. I left a Miss Sophia Worsley at the altar."

Colin could not help it. His jaw fell open, his mind unable to take in Jacob's words.

How could he believe it? The coincidence was astronomical, the odds unbelievable. After all the heartache, panic, fury, and anger he had undergone after Isabella had disappeared, leaving only a cryptic note right before their wedding.

Now he was meeting someone from the other side of that coin.

It had been Jacob and not his bride who had absconded, though Beauvale's disappearance was far more dramatic than Isabella's, even with her penchant for the theatrical.

Colin's thoughts were interrupted by a heavy sigh from Jacob.

"I know, I know, you can say nothing worse than what I have already said to myself," he said dully. "I know what you are thinking. I am a cad, and I deserve neither woman."

"That was not what I was thinking," said Colin hastily.

The last couple was leaving the restaurant now. *They were alone, which was all to the good if this conversation continued in this vein,* thought Colin.

"No," said Jacob perceptively. "But I wasn't far off, was I?"

Colin laughed, dissipating the tension. "Well, no, if I am honest. I cannot imagine the pain that your decision, though right for yourself and your wife, caused to Miss Worsley."

Which was a lie. He could imagine it. He had lived it this last week—though strangely, the pain had dulled rather quickly.

As soon as he had started on the journey with Miss Olivia Lymington.

Jacob's expression was a mixture of sadness and frustration. "If I could have prevented that pain, I…well, that is not entirely true. I should have called the wedding off months before. I kept postponing it, you know, yet she did not expect a thing."

Ye gods, it was worse than he thought! Should he have known Isabella had no intention of following through on their marriage? Was he a fool not to have noticed the signs?

"You see, I knew I was in love with Elizabeth and not Sophia," said Jacob heavily. "Knew it before either of them, and I was a cad attempting to keep both of them happy. I should have done the honorable thing, but I still consider leaving her at the altar honorable. Better that than entering into a marriage I knew would not make anyone happy."

Colin was not entirely sure about that.

To be standing before God at the altar, all of one's family and acquaintances behind you about to watch you become man and wife, and then for that person to suddenly disappear…

Colin shivered. The very thought caused hot shame to rush through his body.

Thank God no one had discovered the truth about his 'wedding' to Isabella. It would not be long before he would have her before an altar, and they really would be man and wife. Then they could begin a life together that would make his parents' marriage look warm.

"I…I am not sure whether I would consider abandoning her at the altar to be the honorable thing," Colin found himself saying in a low voice. "That poor girl."

"I know, I know," said Jacob.

Colin remembered the look of deep affection between Jacob and his wife before she went upstairs to their room. That kiss on the forehead, so tender, so instinctive.

Yes, it was easy to understand how Jacob could not walk away from that.

"Even at that last minute, I believe I did the right thing," Jacob said with a wry smile. "Though not everyone will see it that way. Still, I think that heartbreak in the short term was far superior to simply lying and continue on with it. Would she not have been far more unhappy, Miss Worsley, I mean, if I had lied and pretended to care for her for the rest of our lives?"

Colin opened his mouth but then closed it again. It had not occurred to him.

Was that what Isabella had attempted to do?

In short, was Isabella attempting to break off their wedding because she knew he did not love her, and presumably, she did not love him?

The rage of being abandoned by her without a word rose in Colin's heart. It was insupportable what Isabella had put him through.

But this was not the time to worry about such things. His friend was looking downcast, and it was not his job to cast judgment about such things. *What sort of an expert was he?*

"Well, whatever the morals of the situation, I am sure of one thing," Colin said in a teasing voice.

Jacob looked up nervously. "What is that?"

"I am sure Miss Sophia Worsley will never get over you."

Colin had not expected Jacob to laugh.

"Oh, I am not so sure of that," said the married man with a cheerful grin. "I wouldn't worry too much if I were you."

Colin raised an eyebrow. "No?"

Jacob shook his head. "No, within six months she married, a love match with an earl! A man significantly older than her, too, after parting with his mistress of almost seven years."

It was all Colin could do to keep his face calm. "You don't mean—"

"The Earl of Marnmouth!" Jacob laughed, all tension now gone from his features. "That Sophia likes a bit of drama if you ask me."

Their cigars had entirely gone out, ignored due to the intrigue of their conversation, but Colin was not worried. He had been entertained enough to keep his mind from the desire of the tobacco.

"Well," he said, leaning back in his chair, "I suppose that shows you how little I know about marriage!"

He had intended his words to be a jest only, but his friend was looking at him a little too shrewdly for his liking. "I wouldn't say that. Your Isabella looks very happy, and I have to say, she is far more pleasant than she ever had been when I encountered her here in Bath or London."

Colin tried not to smile. *So, he had noticed something then but had not thought so wildly as to guess at the truth!*

"I hope you do not mind me saying that, of course," added Jacob with a grin. "But I speak as I find. She is much improved."

The smile Colin was trying to suppress broke free. "I do not think she is any different, and she certainly doesn't look any different."

"Oh, that," said Jacob, waving his hand as though to bat aside Colin's words. "'Tis not about how she looks, though she is pretty, I grant you. No, it's something deeper than that. She is much calmer, sweeter, more interested in others. She would never have put up with Elizabeth talking about our two children like that for hours on end. I'm usually the only person that is that interested!"

Colin laughed and did not reply immediately. Yes, the Lymington twin sisters were vastly different. *How had it taken him this long to understand that?*

The woman he knew as Isabella was just a pretty face.

But if he had wanted to get to know her, perhaps he would have spent more time in London rather than in Scotland!

It was strange to have it so clear before him now that it was too late. It was not merely Isabella's fault that she had disappeared before their wedding. It was his, too. He had not invested in this marriage, and now he knew Olivia, *really knew her.*

"Goodness, we should be off to bed, too, you know," said Jacob as he glanced at his pocket watch.

"Yes, of course," Colin said automatically, rising to his feet.

Though Jacob would never know it, he had served Colin well. His story, his thinking had helped Colin to make a decision that he would never have believed possible.

Tomorrow, when he found Isabella, he would not be forcing her to accompany him to a church.

No. He would be on bended knee, asking her to free him from their engagement, and then...

Then he would propose to Olivia. Colin smiled. She was the one he wanted, the woman who would bring him the most happiness. He needed her—more than he had ever known.

"You all right, old chap?"

Colin blinked. Jacob had started walking away from their table but had halted as the duke had not followed him.

Colin smiled. "Better than ever."

CHAPTER FIFTEEN

ISABELLA. THEY WERE but yards from her, standing outside the Lymington house in Bath, where Olivia was sure her twin sister must be. She appeared to be correct, for the shutters had been removed, and there was a light inside at this early morning hour.

"You are sure she's here?"

Olivia swallowed to calm her voice before she replied, "As sure as I can possibly be."

She had not looked at him as she spoke. She could not. In mere moments, that door would open, and the Duke of Larnwick's real bride would appear.

And this, whatever this had been between them, would be over.

Over before it had even begun.

"And if she is not here?"

Olivia heard the strain in his voice. *If they had been through all of this for nothing...*

"Then we will have to think of a different approach," she said as firmly as she could.

Her voice belied the panic starting to rise in her. It had been minutes since she had knocked. If there was someone in there, surely they would have come to the door by now?

What if she was wrong? What if Isabella was leading them on a wild goose chase, and she had never come to Bath at all?

It would be just like her, Olivia thought sadly, *to lie to the hotel manager in Brighton to attempt to throw them off the scent.*

"Right," said Colin quietly. "A different approach."

He seemed…almost nonchalant about finding her. This did not match the ardent desire she had seen in him to find his missing bride.

It was almost as though that desire had disappeared or been placed elsewhere.

Olivia's memory stirred with a remembrance of how the duke had been when they had first discovered that Isabella had disappeared.

"I cannot recall ever being so upset!"

And yet, the gentleman before her now seemed almost not to care whether he found his future bride or not. It was most disorientating.

"Should I knock again?" Olivia began, but she halted as a sound hit her ears.

The sound of footsteps, and not outside, but inside the house.

Olivia's heart twisted, and her stomach lurched. This was the moment they discovered, once and for all, why Miss Isabella Lymington decided marrying a duke was not for her.

The door opened, and there stood a mirror image of herself. *Isabella.*

"Wh-Olivia! Larnwick!" Isabella's mouth fell open. "What on earth, you can't be here!"

Olivia could feel, instinctively, that Colin was expanding with indignation at this rude greeting, and she stepped forward hastily. "Can we come in, Bella, and—"

"No!" There was a look of real panic on her face as Isabella attempted to shut the door. Olivia had already, as a precaution, placed a foot across the threshold. "Go away. I said in my note I wasn't coming back!"

"Bella, be reasonable and let us have this discussion inside," said Olivia, casting a look at Colin behind her, who was standing stock-still, staring at the pair of them.

Her heart sank. She knew what he must be thinking. Now that he had the pair of them before him, together again, he was surely realizing that it was Isabella that he felt affection for. *No one ever saw the two of them together and chose her.*

"Go away, Livvy!" Isabella was beside herself.

Olivia had never seen her in such a passion.

"I will be gone soon, so you can tell our parents I have done naught but stay here a few days, I shall have my own rooms in just—unhand me!"

It was not her twin sister she shouted at, but Colin Vaughn, Duke of Larnwick. Without a word, without even seeming to realize what he was doing, he had stepped forward, grabbed the arm of the woman who was supposed to be his wife, and pushed her into the house.

Olivia followed and shut the door behind her with relief. *The last thing they wanted was witnesses to this sort of reunion.*

"Let go of me, you blaggard!"

Olivia sighed before she turned around to see what should have been the happy couple. She knew that tone of Isabella's.

The Lymington's Bath house was resplendent, even for them. The hallway was large, with a sweeping staircase and beautiful stone flooring.

"We have come a long way to see you, Isabella," said Colin in a low voice, so sharp Isabella halted her protests. "And you are going to listen to us."

Olivia almost rolled her eyes. *Had the man any idea how to speak to Isabella?*

"His Grace means," she said hastily, stepping forward once again as a mediator, seemingly her only role, "that we need to speak with you, Isabella."

Colin released his grip on her, but he did not step away. Isabella, Olivia noticed, did not move but looked at him with wary eyes. She was intrigued to see Isabella looked not only genuinely surprised to see them but a little anxious, too.

She was hiding something. Olivia had known that look for twenty-one years. *But what could she possibly be hiding now?*

"You have to go," said Isabella, and this time her voice was low, as though she was afeared of being overheard.

Colin snorted. "Go? We are not going anywhere, Miss Lymington, until we have some *explanations*."

He was breathing heavily, and Olivia tried not to notice just how handsome he looked when riled. It was not her place to do so. Not now the happy couple had been reunited at least.

She watched them. Isabella, looking up in fear and respect. Colin, looking down in a sort of wild passion, the anger of the last few days raining down on her.

Olivia shivered. *Was it wrong to wish that such desire, such jealousy, was for her?* All this passion was for Isabella, and the irony was that she did not seem to want it.

She would never have run from Colin. Except…except she had certainly pulled away. They had shared something beautiful, and she had drawn back.

"Can we…can we just forget that this ever happened?"

"You need to tell me," Colin began in a fierce voice.

"Keep your voice down!" Isabella interrupted. "Be quiet, can't you! And go away, Larnwick, I cannot possibly marry you!"

Olivia looked hastily at him. She had expected to see pain, or at the very least, irritation. But there was nothing there but curiosity.

"Isabella Lymington, you have led me on a pretty dance for months, years!" he said, taking a step toward her. "You owe me an—"

"Why don't we all step into the drawing room," suggested Olivia, hoping to defuse the tension. "We can calmly discuss…"

"No, you cannot possibly stay here. You need to go!" Isabella looked pleadingly toward her sister and then glanced at the staircase. "Please, just go!"

Olivia swallowed her frustrations and tried to think about how to extricate them from this situation. How did the Duke of Larnwick want this conversation to go? And why did Isabella keep insisting that she could not speak to them, or more, that she *could not* marry him?

"What is going on here!" exploded Colin, his voice bellowing in the hallway. "What about all the promises! You owe me an explanation, Isabella, and I'm not leaving until I get one."

"Keep your voice down!"

"Why?" At Olivia's word, both Isabella and Colin turned to her. Olivia had expected to feel self-conscious, but she didn't. Something had clicked in her mind. "Isabella, why should we keep our voices down? We are the only ones here, aren't we?"

Isabella's eyes met hers, and Olivia knew there was someone else here, but neither twin was given the opportunity to speak.

"After all your promises, I need to know why you wouldn't commit to being my wife."

It was not merely anger in his words now, but pain. Frustration. The fear of rejection, Olivia could hear them all, and her heart broke for him.

"It is just the two of you who have come? On your own?" Isabella asked, her gaze flickering between her sister and her betrothed. "You must have stayed the night somewhere, do people think—"

"They all think she's you or that you are her," snapped Colin. "A fine dance you've led us, halfway across the country!"

Isabella put a hand to her face, clearly in shock, and Olivia could not help but be surprised. They had done it all for her, to keep her secret, and she had assumed Isabella would in a tiny way be grateful.

"I..." Isabella's voice failed her, and she swallowed before continuing, "I wrote in the note exactly. I told you I could not marry you, and that's all I have to say! Please leave!"

"Look," he said, taking a step toward her. "Olivia and I have traveled a long way for this conversation, and you cannot escape us now!"

Olivia tried not to show her sadness. Just two days ago, they had spent a night together, and now she was Miss Lymington. It was cruel being forced to watch this reunion.

She caught his gaze and saw by the flush across his cheeks he was thinking the same thing. *It all could have been so different. And yet…*

"Isabella," she said softly. Her twin looked at her, eyes full of fear. "Isabella, why don't you tell us why you cannot marry the Duke of Larnwick? You have to admit, it is a bit strange to be engaged to a man for two years and keep putting off the wedding with no reason!"

Olivia had never seen her twin look so anxious. *What was going on?*

"I…I don't know how to say," began Isabella in a quiet voice, but then said, "No!"

Her gaze had moved to a point behind Olivia and Colin, which must have been why they had not noticed the sound of footsteps on the stairs. As they whirled around, they saw a figure halfway down the staircase.

"What is going on?" asked the man mildly.

Olivia's mouth fell open. It was… "Harold!"

No–no, this could not be happening. Was this a bad dream, a nightmare she had slipped into at the hotel? Because he could not be here. The last time she had seen him, it was in the arms of Isabella…

"Who the devil are you?" Colin snapped.

"Harold Jones," he said in that calm voice. "And who are you?"

"Colin," hissed Olivia, stepping forward and taking his arm. *She had to warn him, had to tell him that…*

"I am Miss Isabella Lymington's betrothed," said Colin stiffly.

Harold laughed. "What, betrothed to my wife? Be reasonable, man."

Olivia's breath was entirely stolen. She could not breathe, could not move, could only stare at the sister she had known better than anyone else in the world.

Harold Jones' wife?

This truly was a nightmare. As though it was not enough that she'd succumbed to Colin's embraces, now she was standing in her parents' home and hearing that the man she thought had loved her had married Isabella.

But no, that was all over. That had already happened. When Isabella and Harold had been found, they had been forced apart by their parents, and that was two years ago.

Wasn't it?

"The devil she is, man," said Colin heavily, taking a step toward him.

"Colin," said Olivia weakly.

Colin halted.

"Colin, this is…this is the man I was engaged to," Olivia said quietly. *She could hardly believe she was saying this.* "The man who left me for Isabella."

She had expected him to show her pity, to even pull her into his arms and comfort her.

But the Duke of Larnwick did nothing of the sort. Looking between them in horror and surprise, he said slowly, "Is…is this some sort of joke to all of you?"

"Harold," murmured Isabella, stepping around the duke and into the waiting arms of her husband. "The only reason we were parted was because my parents were angry, and so was Olivia, and rightly so. Olivia, you cannot understand what it is to fall in love with a man who is meant to love your sister!"

Olivia's mouth fell open. *She was not dreaming because even her mind could not have imagined such madness.*

"Why did you not saying anything?" Colin stared at the woman who was supposed to be his bride. "Why allow the façade of our match to continue?"

Isabella looked wretched but spoke strongly and, Olivia noticed, without that petulant affectation she had gained over the last year or so. *Was everything Isabella had been an act?*

"I did not know what to do," said the newly revealed Mrs. Jones. "The deeper I fell into the lies, the more complicated they became to keep right!"

"I told her years ago to come clean," said Harold with an almost apologetic look.

Olivia's breath caught in her throat, and Colin immediately noticed the same thing.

"Years ago?" Colin took another step closer to the seemingly happy couple. "Years – how long have you been married?"

Isabella drew herself up and said in a voice both proud and embarrassed, "Almost two years."

It was all Olivia could do to remain upright. The world was spinning so quickly, and yet no one else seemed to be affected by it.

How was it possible that her sister could be married? Married for almost two years? No hint had been given!

She looked instinctively at Colin. She knew he would take this hard, consider this not only a betrayal of him but of everyone who had waited to celebrate their nuptials.

"Two years," he said darkly, which Olivia knew was a warning sign.

"I am sure if we sat down to discuss this," said Harold in a soothing voice, "we—"

"No." Colin's voice was dark, low, dangerous in a way Olivia had never heard before. "I'm leaving. Come on, Olivia."

In that instant, she was torn. She felt betrayed. Harold Jones may not have stirred in her the same emotions that Colin did, but she had believed at the time that he was enamored with her. *They had been engaged, and now he was married to her sister?*

"Come, Olivia."

Colin took her arm in his and marched her away. It was only when the door closed behind her and the wintery Bath wind whipped at her face that Olivia realized they had left.

"You knew."

Olivia blinked. "I beg your pardon?"

Colin was glaring with righteous indignation. "You knew! I should have seen it from the start, your father offering me to you? You wanted to use this trip to…to seduce me!"

Olivia could not believe what she was hearing. After all this heartache she had suffered!

And even now, he believed such despicable things about her?

"Why would I lie about all this?" she said defensively, conscious that they were having a heated debate in the street. "Why would I put myself through such misery!"

"I think you and your sister planned that at least one of you would get a duke," Colin shot back. "Even if it couldn't be her."

This was all going wrong. "You have to believe me. I knew as little about this as you!"

But Olivia could see in his eyes that he did not believe her. "How did you know about Brighton, then? About the exact place she was staying there, and here in Bath!"

"She's my twin sister!" Olivia said dismissively. "We have lived almost the same life. I know how she thinks!"

But the duke was looking at her with disappointment. "I trusted you, and the whole time, you've been playing me for a fool. Goodbye, Miss Olivia Lymington."

He walked away, and Olivia did not attempt to follow him.

Despite her broken heart, there would be no happy ending for the second Lymington twin.

CHAPTER SIXTEEN

COLIN DRAINED THE glass, then looked at it in surprise. It was not supposed to be empty.

The damned bottle was empty, too. How had that happened?

He looked around, though he knew he was alone. Colin swallowed. If no one else had drunk from the bottle, then it was him. That was unlike him. He was not usually one to drink, but then, he had plenty of cause to.

"I trusted you, and the whole time, you've been playing me for a fool. Goodbye, Miss Olivia Lymington."

Colin remembered the look on Olivia's face. *Had she known?* Of course she had. It was ridiculous to think a twin sister would not have known that her sister had been married for almost two years!

He opened his eyes, and the hotel room swam into view. It was soulless without her. How had Miss Olivia Lymington played on his emotions so easily? If he had not fallen in love with the elder twin, he had expected nothing special from the younger.

His heart clenched. *But she was* special.

His heart hardened. She had utterly taken him in with her wiles, her lies, her ability to twist the truth and lead him on a merry dance across England.

It could not be clearer that Olivia and her sister had planned the entire thing.

He leaned forward and picked up the empty bottle of wine as though discovering it for the first time. *Of course. He had drunk the wine.*

That was why his head felt fuzzy, and his ability to see was starting to blur.

Olivia. What a mastermind she was, Colin thought dully, allowing the bottle of wine to crash onto the floor, smashing into pieces.

Christ alive, it was embarrassing how obvious it was in hindsight.

It was a small mercy that absolutely no one knew about it.

Dear God. He had been to Brighton and now Bath with a woman he called his wife, Isabella.

But that was not possible. Isabella was married. It would all come out soon, and it would be assumed, and rightly so, that it was Olivia with whom he had been traveling!

Colin laughed darkly in the gloom of the hotel room. *Well, it was a dangerous gamble for Miss Olivia Lymington to be sure, and he was not entirely sure whether it had come right for her in the end.*

What was she going to do about that particular piece of gossip?

The door opened, and Colin looked blearily to see a footman standing in the doorway.

"I beg your pardon, Your Grace, but I heard a..." The footman's voice trailed away as he took in the disheveled duke, the darkness of the room, and the smashed bottle of wine. "Ah. I see there has been an accident."

Well done, Colin thought. No point accusing one's guests of being willfully destructive.

"Yes, an accident," he said, finding his tongue challenging to manage around the last word. "Whoops."

The footman had evidently seen his fair share of intoxicated gentlemen. Within a minute, three candles had been lit around the room, the glass was swept up, and the footman about to leave.

"Wait."

The servant hesitated. "Yes, Your Grace."

Colin smiled. "Another bottle of your finest, please."

He watched the footman's gaze move to the carpet and then to the dustpan and brush in his hands, still full of the evidence of the first bottle.

"I am a duke," said Colin, hating himself. *This wasn't who he was! He didn't pull rank on a poor servant!* "I am paying you, and I order you to bring me another bottle of wine. Charge me double. And for the carpet."

The footman nodded and closed the door behind him.

He would pay for that in the morning. Well, what did it matter? He had money, and it wasn't doing any good in the bank. Besides, he had thought it would be spent on a wife, on extravagant plans for their home in Scotland, on children.

Nothing to spend it on now.

There was a knock on the door. *The footman was quick*, Colin thought. *Far quicker than he had expected.*

"Come," he barked.

The door opened and revealed Jacob Beauvale with a bottle of wine in his hands.

"Hallo there," he said cheerily, "I saw you come back to the hotel without your wife, and when I saw the footman with the wine, I thought I would deliver—dear God, Larnwick, what has happened?"

Colin laughed bitterly. It was ill news indeed that an acquaintance could tell within a moment that something dreadful had happened just by the look on his face. He would have to be careful to regulate his expressions when he finally left here.

"Is it that obvious?"

Jacob stepped into the room and closed the door behind him. "I mean to say, the wine bottle was a clue, but you look as though someone has died! Isabella is quite fine, isn't she?"

Colin held out a hand for the bottle. If he was not mistaken, his friend hesitated before handing it over to him.

"Well?" he said, stepping forward. "Is Isabella well?"

Colin blinked at the bottle. *Was it the same one?* He could hardly recall.

"Larnwick!"

"Yes, yes," he said irritably, waving a hand and indicating the man should sit down. "Yes, she's quite well. She's with her husband."

There was a look of utter confusion on Jacob's face as he sank into the armchair.

"I don't understand," he said with that rather charming directness Colin had always admired in him. "Isabella with her husband? So where is she? What's going on?"

Colin hesitated, but only for a moment. The truth would be coming out soon, wouldn't it? What better person to tell than someone he knew would not twist the truth for his own ends, and if he told the tale, would at least tell it faithfully.

"Isabella and I are not married," Colin said heavily.

Jacob's mouth opened, but he closed it quickly and narrowed his eyes at his friend. "You mean…do you mean, you've eloped? You have not married yet?"

Colin did not answer. He was too focused on attempting to open the bottle of wine, which was putting up a tremendous fight. It was only after Jacob tutted and took the bottle from him that Colin realized he had been trying to open it with his finger.

"Here," Jacob said, picking up the corkscrew lying on the bed, opening the bottle, and pouring into each glass. "Take this, drink it down, and then tell me what the hell is going on."

Colin took the glass but did not immediately drink. Instead, he held the glass aloft and said, "To Isabella, the bride of two years ago."

He poured the contents of the glass down his throat. *God, this really was an excellent bottle of wine. He couldn't begin to think how expensive it was.*

When he looked up, Jacob was just staring.

"What?" Colin said defensively. "You think I should have given her a greater toast?"

"What on earth are you talking about, man?" It was not in Jacob's nature to be so sharp, Colin knew. "Christ, man, are you drunk?"

Colin smiled sadly. "I wish I was."

It would do little good to tell the full story, he knew, but he had to tell someone. He had been sat here, in this room for hours, with nothing to do but think about the last few days. Those thoughts had brought him no comfort. Perhaps revealing them to Jacob would. Perhaps he would have an insight Colin had missed.

"Jacob, my dear friend, I do not intend to be obtuse," he said with a hiccup. "Well, maybe I do a little. But you see, the whole story is so complex, so ridiculous…"

Jacob picked up the wine bottle and moved it to the other side of his chair.

"You have had enough," he said with a frown. "Now, for goodness sake, what is going on?"

Colin took a deep breath. "The woman you spent yesterday evening with?"

Jacob nodded. "Yes, Isabella."

It was all Colin could do not to laugh. "It wasn't Isabella. It was Olivia."

He was not entirely sure what reaction he had been expecting, let alone hoping for, so Colin found he laughed when Jacob's eyes widened.

"What? Y-You're eloping with the twin?"

Colin found that he probably should have done that in the first place.

"Her sister, an exact match. Why not marry her?"

Second choice. Oh, how Olivia hated that term. He had seen the fury in her soul, and he had loved it. He had loved her.

"Oh, it's just such a horrible tangle and mess, the pair of them," Colin said bitterly. "Those Lymington twins, they will be the death of me!"

As he looked up, he could see that Jacob was utterly lost. "I think you may have to go back to the beginning and explain properly, and I will need this glass of wine, won't I?"

Colin grinned. *Well, he deserved that.* "'Tis all very simple when it comes down to it. Isabella was the one I was engaged to for years, but it turns out, as I have discovered, that was all rather fruitless. She is already married, has been for two years."

Jacob's face was a picture of shock. "But why would she keep it a secret?"

"I do not believe the gentleman in question was particularly well off," said Colin heavily, and then with a little spite that he knew was entirely unwarranted, "I do not believe he was a gentleman at all."

Jacob gulped a little more wine.

"And, of course, it gets more complicated."

"It does?"

Colin nodded. "To make it even worse, he was once engaged to the other twin. Olivia. The one you dined with yesterday."

"This is all getting dashed confusing," said Jacob with a wry smile, draining his glass and pouring himself another one. "Too complicated, if you ask me."

Colin laughed. "You try being in the middle of it! It's more than I can cope with, I can tell you. So I have spent the last three days or so chasing one twin who was already married, with the other twin who I think was trying to land me for herself."

"Was she, by Jove?"

"I should have known," said Colin heavily. The power of the bottle of wine was starting to cool, and his thoughts were starting to make more sense as he meandered through them. "I mean, I guessed she had a little fancy for me. We have spent more time together since I came down to London, and I saw how she looked at me..." Colin swallowed. "And how I looked at her. Beautiful, but nothing more would have come of it."

He had barely noticed her, considered her nothing more than an extension of her twin. Little wonder he had never bothered to find out more about her, realized what a precious jewel she was…

"Sounds to me like you have the perfect solution."

Colin's head jerked upward. "I do?"

Jacob nodded. "I'm surprised you can't see it yourself. You've fallen in love with the unmarried twin, so marry her. Isn't that what you want?"

Dear God, if only it were that simple. "It has all been secrets and lies, Beauvale. They have led me a merry dance up the aisle."

Jacob laughed but stopped when he saw Colin's face. "Yes, but isn't that the point? You could still go up the aisle with one. The one you care for, by the sound of it."

It was such a bizarre idea that Colin gave it some thought. He certainly felt affection for Olivia, strong affection. He had called it love in the privacy of his mind, but was it enough? Were his feelings for her enough to ignore the lies, the trickery?

Colin shook his head. "One Lymington twin pretended to wish to marry me while she was married to another. The other sought only to catch me for my title and fortune. She has no affection for me."

Jacob frowned. "I do not know what you're talking about. The woman I saw yesterday was in love with you."

In love with him? Colin could not believe it. Olivia had no affection for him. She had proved that with the way she had acted.

Unless…unless he had got everything wrong.

"You have to believe me. I knew as little about this as you!"

"Do you mean that?"

Jacob nodded. "Olivia, the woman I saw yesterday? She is besotted with you, Larnwick. I have never seen anyone other than Elizabeth with that sort of devotion. If you've lost her entirely, that's one thing, but if there's a chance to get her back, shouldn't you take it?"

CHAPTER SEVENTEEN

OLIVIA CLOSED HER eyes. "This is like a nightmare I cannot wake from."

The soft chaise longue she was lying on in the drawing room was a comfort, at least. It was furniture she knew well. Her mother had purchased it ten years ago, more?

Many a wet afternoon in Bath had been spent here with a good book or a piece of embroidery, or, more likely, listening to Isabella go on about how many pretty gowns she was going to have when she finally came out into society.

Olivia opened her eyes to see that same sister, somehow looking much wiser, seated on the sofa opposite.

"I do not think so," said Isabella lightly.

Olivia tried, she really did. She knew her sister was not being deliberately difficult. But it was rather a strain to be told things were not bad when it was her doing in the first place!

"Really?" Olivia said, sitting upright and glaring at her sister. "You do not think it is that bad? Perhaps that is because you are the one creating all the problems!"

"This would have been so simple," said Isabella calmly, "if everyone had not reacted so badly to the fact that I fell in love with Harold!"

Olivia opened her mouth but closed it again. That statement, evenly spoken, was a difficult one to disagree with. It was evident by their marriage that Isabella and Harold had a deep and abiding affection.

When they had been found, of course, dining in a hotel and not yet married…well, anyone would have been shocked.

For Mr. and Mrs. Lymington, it was an outrage. Isabella was never to see him again, and the whole thing would be hushed up.

But while Olivia could not help but privately agree that was where the trouble had all started, she was not going to give Isabella any credit for the thought, not when she had caused the entire disaster.

"Perhaps if you had not fallen in love with my betrothed in the first place," Olivia said, her words intending to sting, "this would not have happened!"

Not waiting for a response, Olivia sank back onto the chaise longue, though its comforting softness was not sufficient to distract her from all she had learned over the last day.

Isabella, married. Married to Harold! Married for two years.

And Colin believing her to be some sort of harlot, tempting him along on the journey with the express desire to bed him and wed him!

Well, it was ridiculous! It was shameful that he would even think such a thing!

Olivia bit her lip.

"I think you and your sister planned that at least one of you would get a duke. Even if it couldn't be her."

His words pained her, but she could not judge him entirely. It was all such a mess, one that she had been convinced could be solved as soon as they found Isabella.

"You see, this is why the full truth is not entirely helpful," said Isabella in a determined voice. Olivia did not look up as she continued, "If you and Mother and Father had just left me alone if you had found us not twelve hours later, then I would have been married. I could have continued with the life I wanted and have been happy with Harold."

Olivia looked over at her sister and realized something with a jolt.

The simpering fool of a sister she had been forced to live with for the last two years had gone. The silly way of speaking, that rather irritating high-pitched laugh she had developed, the rudeness, the idiocy…

All had gone. All had been part of the act, a way to keep other gentlemen away and perhaps even encourage the Duke of Larnwick to break off the suit.

Olivia almost laughed.

It was all because Isabella was not Isabella Lymington. She was Mrs. Harold Jones.

It was hard to believe, even with the evidence right there before her. The entire thing was so tangled. She was not entirely sure whether she would be able to explain it.

"You really love him?" The quiet words escaped her before she could stop herself.

Isabella nodded, and her whole face came alive. "Oh, yes. More than I could have guessed. Even when he revealed he was not rich, that he was penniless, I—"

"What?" Olivia sat up hurriedly. "What do you mean, *penniless*? When he and I…well, when we were engaged, he was relatively wealthy!"

It was one of the reasons, she thought wryly, *their parents had been so eager for the match.* No title, to be sure, but then Olivia was only the second twin. The second choice. Why not give her a marriage to a man who appeared scandal-free and had a large fortune?

"Yes," said Isabella, nodding with a sad expression. "Yes, it was true then. But in the weeks before your…your intended marriage, he lost almost all of it. A speculation, he tells me. He brought nothing to our marriage but himself, and of course, no one knows I am married, so Father did not give him my thirty thousand pounds dowry. That was, until…I had no choice, you see. I had to keep putting it off."

"Dear God," Olivia breathed. "You…you have been putting off your marriage to Colin until we turned twenty-one!"

How could she have been so blind? Why hadn't she seen it at once?

Isabella knew she would not be given her dowry if their parents discovered the illicit marriage, the one they had worked so hard to prevent.

But they needed the money. It could not be more clear if Harold had lost all his wealth in a speculation, that they could not live together without money.

And so Isabella, with that clever wit Olivia had almost forgotten, had strung on that poor man over and over again. Just moving the wedding a few months…then a few more – and then a few more, until just weeks ago, they both turned one and twenty.

And came into their fortunes.

"We came of age, and our dowries became our own," Olivia said slowly. "That was what you were waiting for."

Isabella nodded with no hint of shame, though she did not meet her sister's eyes.

"Yes," she said quietly. "I am not proud of it, but the deception was necessary. I love him too much to let him go, Olivia, and now with the thirty thousand pounds, we can afford to live together as husband and wife."

Olivia stared. Such deception, all for the love of a man once engaged to herself!

She had expected anger to rise once again; that the fury she had felt, the confusion and upset which had overwhelmed her heart when she had seen Harold, would return in full force.

But instead, she felt…strange. Astonished that Isabella could have kept up such a ruse for so long. A little impressed, despite herself, that her twin sister had been able to think of a solution to a problem that was, admittedly, of her own making.

And proud. Rightly or wrongly, no matter the morals of such a situation, all the silliness Isabella had inflicted on those around her had been an act.

"Having Larnwick around was like some sort of shield," Isabella continued. "I would not be forced to suffer through any other gentleman's attentions, and he was quite pleasant, really. I did worry, of course, that his heart might be touched, but I really was as disagreeable as I could be."

Olivia smiled. "That you were."

"And now I have my dowry," said Isabella, utterly missing the irony in her sister's voice. "Harold has always wanted to open a shop, perhaps in Wells or Gloucester. A little shop, just for the two of us."

Horror filled Olivia's heart. *A little shop?* A Lymington, the eldest Lymington daughter with a dowry of thirty thousand pounds, opening a shop in a backwater town where no one of any breeding or society would venture?

And then she looked at the glow of happiness on her sister's face and felt ashamed. *Who was she to be so judgmental, to assume that such a life could bring no one happiness?* Who was she to say that wasn't the right way to live one's life?

It was not as though they came from a great lineage, after all. Their father had done much the same and built a trade empire that gave his eldest daughter the power of choice, a very valuable thing indeed.

And he was happy, wasn't he? With their mother by his side, they had built something far more impressive than a business. They had built a family. And they had been happy as children, had wanted for nothing, including love.

One could find happiness, Olivia mused, *but sometimes you had to make it.*

She sighed. "I understand going to our parents would not have ended particularly well for you both. But you could have told me. You could have confided in me years ago."

Isabella raised an eyebrow in that rather startling way that Olivia hated. She knew she did it as well. Sometimes it really was like looking into a mirror.

"Really? After all the fuss that you and our parents made after we tried to elope?"

Olivia's mouth fell open at those words. When she looked back on those painful few days, it was always as a bride who had been jilted, as a sister who had been betrayed.

But hearing Isabella speak so affectionately of her husband, seeing them together...

"I am sorry," Olivia said, a little awkwardly. "I can see now that the two of you were made for each other."

"I know," said Isabella softly, reaching out a hand and squeezing that of her sister's. "And it was all my idea, of course. Harold wished to tell you, to take you into our confidence at the time. But I was not sure. I could not risk that you would tell."

Olivia squeezed her hand. "I would not have betrayed you, but you did not know that."

Isabella's eyes filled with tears. "I was so afraid. I thought Mother and Father would attempt to separate us, and I was terrified that I would lose him."

Olivia could do nothing but nod.

"So we have tried to make the best of it over the last few years," said Isabella with a sniff, "though it has been difficult. We have been so much apart."

It was clear Isabella needed to share the loneliness she had experienced. But as her twin continued about their secret assignations, Olivia found her thoughts meandered.

"...but now we can be open," said Isabella with a heavy sigh. Her eyes twinkled. "I really am not so silly as everyone thinks, you know. When did you fall in love with Larnwick?"

Olivia flushed. "What nonsense! Why would you think such a thing?"

But Isabella was not to be distracted. "I am your twin sister. You knew something was wrong when I kept postponing my marriage to Larnwick, though you did not know why."

Olivia swallowed. It felt wrong, somehow, to speak of these emotions.

"He is in love with the idea of me."

"But would you tell him if you loved him?" Isabella was looking at her closely.

"He no longer trusts me," said Olivia sadly. "Why would he believe anything I said?"

Chapter Eighteen

Colin took a long, deep breath, but it did nothing for his nerves. It did not help that his hangover was utterly dreadful. He could not remember the last time he had managed to get himself so blinding drunk, *which was, he supposed, the point.*

Still. It was rotten bad luck that he had managed to get himself so utterly pickled right before he realized that he was so besotted with Olivia that he would do anything to have her.

That second bottle of wine with Jacob did explain the wild idea he had concocted.

The important thing, Colin told himself, *was not to look down.* Looking down would be the end of it because if he tripped and the scarf he had wrapped around his face to disguise himself shifted, he would be in serious trouble.

That was why he paid careful attention to his footsteps as he clambered ungracefully up the side of the coach and dropped himself into the driver's seat.

He had never seen the view of a mail coach from here before. Typically, the Duke of Larnwick took his own carriage and was always inside, asleep or chatting with his companions.

With Olivia...

No, he must not lose his head and start thinking of her. No good would come of that! He needed to stay focused, stay alert.

What had the driver said when he had accepted Colin's bargain and pocketed the leather pouch of gold?

"You'll need to make sure the horses know that you are the boss, y'see? They get mighty skittish if they think it's a fool at the reins."

Colin swallowed. He felt like a fool at the moment. What was he doing? He had awoken that morning, head aching and body frustrated that he had not brought Olivia back to this room and made passionate love to her, and the beginnings of a plan had been in his mind.

A foolish plan. He had been an idiot to think this would work, he thought feverishly as he sat in the cool morning air. The street was starting to fill up, even at this early hour, but no one gave a second glance to the man they assumed was the mail coach driver.

Colin tried to slow his breathing. He knew this was a risk, but he had paid the man well—not only to give up his seat on the mail coach but to ensure there was only one passenger.

Olivia.

Even the thought of her was enough to make his knees weak. It was fortunate for Colin that he was seated in this cold, slightly damp coach. *Olivia.* He loved her, he was sure of it now, and he had almost lost her through weakness and foolishness.

"I trusted you, and the whole time, you've been playing me for a fool. Goodbye, Miss Olivia Lymington."

Colin's stomach clenched painfully. That he had said such things! That he had thought them at the time and worse, leveled them at the woman he now realized he loved.

He would have but one opportunity to prove himself. He hardly deserved it, and it pained him to even think of that look Olivia had shot him just before he had walked away.

Colin gritted his teeth. He had been cruel to Olivia just at the moment when she had most needed him and his comfort. He was a blaggard. But hopefully not for long.

As he sat there, waiting in the guise of the mail coach driver, Colin wondered why he had not seen it immediately. *Why had his instincts taken him to such a dark place, assuming that it was, of course, Olivia's betrayal that had brought him to this place and nothing else?*

He should have known that Olivia would never lie to him.

"You have to believe me. I knew as little about this as you!"

The memory of her lying underneath him naked, shivering with pleasure.

When they had made love, he had loved her. He had just not known it then.

Olivia had fallen in love with him, and what had he done?

Shifting on the uncomfortable seat, Colin pulled the hat he had borrowed from the driver lower over his face. The scarf smelled terrible, something like horses, dogs, and a muddy puddle all combined into one.

It was vital Olivia had no comprehension of who was about to take her to London.

His happiness depended on this. He had to get it right, and if he didn't, he was sure to regret it for the rest of his life.

"…and you will wrap up warm, won't you? You never know how freezing those coaches can get."

Colin's ears pricked up, and he stared at the two ladies who had just turned the corner.

Isabella and Olivia. He knew their faces probably better than anyone else's, but only one sparked such joy he was unsure whether he could breathe in her presence.

"You have wrapped me up warmer than our mother ever did," he heard Olivia say, but there was no malice in her words. "Give over, Bella, I am quite warm."

Colin pulled his scarf a little higher up his face.

"And you are sure you want to go back to London?"

Colin watched as the younger twin hesitated.

"There is nothing left for me in Bath," said Olivia quietly. "Nothing but you, and you have your own life now. You don't want a younger sister hanging about the place."

Isabella raised an eyebrow in the precise manner Colin had seen

Olivia do when someone said something that displeased her.

"Nothing for you in London either, I would say," said Isabella shrewdly. "I think you should be taking the coach to Scotland."

Colin watched as Olivia glanced at a carriage on the other side of the road. *Dear God, there was a carriage to Scotland? What if she decided to go to Scotland instead?*

It would be a rather marvelous demonstration of her affection for him, to be sure, but he would lose sight of her in an instant!

But Olivia sighed. "No. Colin had his chance to listen to me, his opportunity to believe me. But he did not. And you know, I cannot blame him. He has no reason to believe any Lymington daughter!"

Colin felt his heart break. *Even after the way he had treated her, the despicable things he had accused her of, had shouted at her in the street; still, she was determined to believe the best of him, even when there was no reason to do so.*

She looked around as she said, "You know, it is odd."

"What is?" asked Isabella.

Olivia was frowning. Her gaze swept past Colin without a second glance. The scarf and hat must be convincing.

"Do you not think it strange that no one else is getting the London coach?" said Olivia slowly. "I would have expected it to be quiet, true, but not this quiet."

"You know, I had not noticed it, but you are right," Isabella agreed. "it is strange."

His heart was thundering so loudly that Colin was sure they would be able to hear it. Was he going to be found out after all?

Was all that conniving, wheedling, and most importantly, guineas to be futile?

"A perfect excuse to get the best seat before anyone else arrives," Isabella said comfortably. "Go on, in you get. And…and try to explain it all to Father. I do not want him to be disappointed in me."

The sisters embraced. "Do not wait to see me off. I won't be able to bear it."

"Bear it?" said Isabella in surprise, pulling back. "What on earth do you mean?"

Colin watched Olivia dash away a tear. "This is the first time we will be separated."

From what he could see, Isabella brushed her eyes, too. "Don't be silly, Livvy, you'll be here all the time! You know you are welcome here any time. Harold and I will have a room for you."

"Over the shop?"

The two sisters laughed, and Colin was surprised to see just the joy. It was a side to their relationship he had never seen, but then, he had always been so fixated on one of them.

The wrong one.

They appeared to have patched up any differences arisen from the rather wild revelations of the previous day, and if he was in luck, Olivia would remain in a forgiving mood.

She would have to be, if she was going to hear him out.

He coughed, hoping they would take that as a suggestion they should be going, and Colin saw with relief that they did.

"In you go," said Isabella, holding out a hand to help her sister into the carriage.

This was it. There was nothing else he was waiting for, and now he had Olivia in the carriage. He did not stop to think. Instincts took over.

"Yah!"

It was time to put his plan into action, and at first, everything went smoothly. The horses moved forward in a sedate sort of trot, and as the chilly air rushed past him, Colin felt a strange sort of euphoria, heart beating so fast it was almost in time with the numerous hooves before him.

What did he think he was doing? He had to know, had to try to win back Olivia after he had so foolishly pushed her away.

Within moments, Bath had disappeared, and they had entered the countryside. There was still frost in places, and the cattle they passed breathed heavily in the early air.

Colin swallowed and pushed his horses faster. The quicker they could put some distance between themselves and Bath, the better. He did not wish to be disturbed.

Only after another ten minutes, when he was confident they were out of Bath proper, did Colin look for a suitable place. He saw one after another few minutes and gently reined in the horses, slowing them to a stop.

He would find out whether Olivia could forgive him and whether what Jacob saw was real love. *If not…*

Well, he had been away from Scotland too long. Perhaps there he could find peace.

"I say, is there a problem?"

Olivia had poked her head out of the window, and Colin tried not to look at her as he clambered down onto the road.

He needed to stay calm. If he had any hope of explaining himself, he would need his tongue to work and his brain to stay focused.

"Yes," he said shakily.

He opened the door and stepped into the carriage.

"What–what are you doing?" Olivia shrank back to the other side of the coach, her eyes wide at the surprise of his entrance. "What do you want?"

All he could manage was to pull down his scarf, throw away the hat, and choke, "Olivia."

"Colin!" Olivia looked astonished. "Colin, what on earth! Go away!"

"No," said Colin quietly. His calm tone did nothing to quieten her fierceness, something that was making her all the more irresistible. "No, we need to talk."

"We need do no such thing!" Olivia looked furious, her eyes bright and cheeks flushed. "You were the one who wanted me to leave you alone, remember?"

"I will leave you alone," Colin said, heart almost breaking at the thought. "But not until you've heard my piece, Olivia."

"Don't you mean *Isabella*?"

The last word was shot at him like a bullet across his shoulder, and Colin could see the pain in her face. *Christ, he had hurt her.* He should never have allowed his bitterness and confusion at yesterday's revelations to be pointed at her.

"I...I used to," he said heavily, dropping into the seat opposite her. "I once thought she was what I wanted, but it's not. It's you."

If he had thought his words would charm her, he was wrong.

"Oh, I see," said Olivia stiffly. "Always the second choice."

"No! No, I just didn't realize I had made the *wrong* choice," said Colin hastily. How could he make her see? "You...you are not the second choice, Olivia. *You are the right choice.*"

Olivia's frown softened but still looked suspicious. "You are certain you are not just settling after discovering the twin you initially wanted is no longer available?"

It was rather cramped in the coach, even with only the two of them in it, but Colin knew he had to get this right. Moving uncomfortably until he was on bended knee between them, he looked up at the woman who was everything.

"Olivia Lymington, you would be the one settling if you accepted my hand."

He thought for a moment it was not enough. *Should he have made a longer speech? Tried to explain to her just how lost he was without her? Explained that after discovering that there was nothing else in his life but her, that he would be destitute without her?*

Somehow, all of those thoughts and perhaps more seemed spoken, for Olivia smiled. She leaned forward, capturing his lips with hers, and Colin almost wept for the beauty of it.

"I accept," she said quietly. "But only if we go to Scotland first. I want to see this place you love. We can take my parents, and it'll all be above board. Then you can marry me."

Colin laughed, staggered upward, and collapsed on the seat beside her before pulling her into his arms for another kiss.

He could hardly believe it. After all his foolishness, after thinking he just wanted to get the wedding over with, and then hoping it would never go ahead because he realized he did not love Isabella, now he had a woman who was not only beautiful, but more importantly, kind, witty, and entirely his.

How long that kiss lasted, he would never know. Eventually, however, he was forced to break it off and start to descend from the coach.

"Where are you going?"

Colin chuckled at the disappointed voice of his beloved. "Back to Bath. I have only paid for the use of the mail coach for an hour or so!"

"Well then," said Olivia, getting out of the coach herself. "We had better make the most of it."

Utterly unable to believe his eyes, Colin watched as Olivia elegantly clambered up to the driver's seat and then patted the space beside her.

"But you can't sit up there with me!" Colin protested, knowing full well he was not going to win this argument. "It will be windy, wet, cold!"

Olivia gave him that look of steel, and he climbed up to sit beside her.

"Yes, it will," she said matter-of-factly, "and it will be with you."

Colin smiled and kissed her deeply, losing himself in the pleasure he could now give and receive with no guilt to his future bride.

Chapter Nineteen

Breathing in the Scottish air, Olivia wondered how she would ever leave. There was something about this place, something that burrowed into your heart and would not let go.

Scotland. It was far more beautiful than she could have imagined. She had heard about it, but it was rather like the wilds of Africa. One heard about them but never expected to go.

Yet here she was, at the top of a mountain with Colin still clambering up.

What she had seen in the last week since she and her parents had journeyed up here to make the engagement official had been beyond her wildest dreams. Scotland was the most incredible country, so wild and alive!

It was heaven compared to London, compared to its noise and smells and gossip. Here, she could be herself. She could be with Colin, though they had not found any time to…

Well. Her parents were here! And there was to be a very small but very important wedding in a few days.

"It has been a while," said a voice heavy with exhaustion, "since I climbed this one!"

Olivia giggled as she turned to watch Colin take the final few steps onto the top.

"A while?" she teased. "I do not think you have ever climbed a mountain in your life."

Colin straightened up as he took in heavy lungfuls of fresh air. "Nonsense, I am just acting like this to make you feel better."

Olivia shook her head with a wry smile as she looked out at the beautiful view. "How do you ever manage to leave this place!"

"You think this is impressive?" Her future husband took her by the hand and pulled her over to the other side of the mountain, the side they had not climbed. "Look at this."

Olivia looked eagerly in the direction that he was pointing and gasped. An entirely different set of hills and mountains had appeared, and just across the valley from them was…

"A waterfall!" Olivia could hardly believe her eyes. "It does not seem possible that there should be so much beauty in such a small part of the world!"

"Small?" said Colin with a laugh. "I dinna ken if Larnwick be that titch!"

It brought her so much joy when Colin spoke in Scots, and Olivia was a little suspicious he was putting on the accent. But she did not mind. Being here with him was like stepping into another world in which she could be truly happy.

They had each other. They always would.

"I will never forget this week," she said softly.

Colin raised an eyebrow. "Really? I hoped that there would be another week, maybe one coming up very soon, that would be in its own way just as memorable."

His gaze made her cheeks burn. She knew what he wanted, and she would not give in to him, not yet. Not until they were officially man and wife.

He was everything she wanted. After feeling so betrayed, so alone in her own family, she had reconciled with Isabella and secured the love of a good man.

"Is this the first mountain we will climb today?" she said eagerly. "Do you have the strength for another?"

She had not expected him to laugh, though it was good-natured. "Mountain? Ye wench, I was only teasin' ye. Mountain? This is a hill, Olivia, nothin' more!"

Olivia's face fell, and she looked out at the loch on one side and the waterfall on the other.

"Really?" It was hard to believe, after all that exertion, that it was only a hill after all. "Where are the mountains?"

Colin stepped forward and pulled her into him, both looking out in the same direction. Olivia gloried in the feeling, his strong arms around her, his chest keeping her safe. There was no one like him.

"Look over there," he said softly, pointing.

Olivia leaned into his arm, breathing in his scent. It was a good thing it was cold today, or else she would be in quite a dangerous position.

"Follow yon line o'trees," Colin continued. "Down the ridge there, and y'see the purple shadow behind it?"

Olivia nodded. "Oh, Colin, they are miles and miles away!"

He laughed softly. "Most of Scotland is miles and miles of this, lass. Miles of it, ready to be explored."

Warmth seeped into her heart, quite at odds with the chilly wind. It was more than she could have ever hoped. She had taken a liking to the tall Scotsman, to be sure, but a duke was not just someone a lady could pick out and decide to have for herself.

Yet she had claimed him.

"Can we go over there?" she said eagerly, her gaze still trained on the mountains that Colin had pointed out.

"Tomorrow."

Colin stepped away, and Olivia turned instinctively like a sunflower, desperate for the sun.

"Tomorrow? Can't we go today?"

He shook his head. "No, the sun will set a lot faster here than you are accustomed to down in the south, lass. We can go over there, but today? We'd have to get down this mountain of yours, across to the castle, take a carriage over…no, 'tis best left 'til tomorrow."

Olivia nodded. *Well, she could not argue with that sort of local knowledge.* Besides, there was still plenty for her to explore in the castle.

Castle! How had the Duke of Larnwick never mentioned to her before, nor any of the Lymington family, that he lived in a castle?

And Larnwick Castle was not just a heap of bricks and ancient history. It was beautiful, carved out of stone. Windows tall and high let light into every room, and Olivia had not yet tired of peeking through doorways to discover fresh delights.

"Well, there isn't a part of Scotland that you've shown me that I haven't enjoyed," said Olivia with a smile. "Every sight is…well, it amazes me. 'Tis hard to believe that you were able to tear yourself away from it and come south where it is so flat, and…and boring!"

Colin grinned. "I never wanted to. Scotland holds my heart, and so do you."

Olivia's heart turned a somersault. *He was hers. All hers.*

"But the time came for the Duke of Larnwick to create heirs," he continued with a mocking smile. "I traveled to London to find a bride, and that, as you well know, was over two years ago. I've been back on and off, but I had to continue down south to harass your wicked sister. I was never going to get any heirs without a wedding first!"

She laughed and wondered whether to speak. There was never any good time to bring up such a topic, she knew that. The temptation to speak earlier had been strong, but she had always put it off.

Olivia had been sure that she would know when to share the secret. *This was not it.*

"I suppose," she said lightly, "every titled man, or every gentleman really, is looking for a way to continue on the family line."

Colin barked a dry laugh. "There is far more pressure to do so when you have a title, I tell you, but I was never in a rush. I found a bride after all, though not the one I expected."

Olivia still felt a pang of jealousy at the mere suggestion of Isabella. It was not her twin sister's fault, not entirely. She should have been more open with her, but Olivia could see why she had not.

"Now, then, that time is past," he said quietly, putting an arm around her and drawing her close. "You are the only one for me. Isabella wasn't right."

"I think she was intentionally most irritating," said Olivia with a laugh.

"And irritating she was, but I suppose I will come to know the true Isabella in time, just as Harold will come to know you. 'Tis a strange sort of family, but I suppose I will get accustomed to it."

Olivia wondered, sometimes, whether he ever would. *Whether she ever would.*

"You *are* the one for me," repeated Colin, misunderstanding her silence. "I am just so relieved you were finally able to forgive me. I only wish I had chosen you from the start!"

Olivia leaned into his embrace, feeling his heartbeat. He was a truly remarkable man, her Colin. He had been faced with an impossible situation, one which had only become more ridiculous as time had gone on.

"I suppose people will now start to see how different Isabella and I are," she mused.

Was that a chuckle from her husband to be? "I don't know. I think with Harold, she'll soften to become more like you."

"And I will toughen up like her?"

"I did not say that," Colin said with a smile.

"'Tis strange, looking back," she said quietly. "I consider the last few years and what Isabella was like during them, and I cannot blame her. Leading a double life to that extreme…it must have been intensely stressful."

"It would certainly have been hard, yes," said Colin quietly with less sympathy for her wayward sister. "But she could have just come clean and told the truth."

There was too much rationality in that statement, Olivia thought. *Isabella was not one to think things through in such a manner.*

No, she just leapt into what her heart wanted, and it had wanted Harold. Only after they had become man and wife had she probably thought of the consequences of her actions, and goodness knows what other alternatives she considered. It was how Isabella was made.

"Well," said Olivia heartily. "All's well that ends well, I suppose. We both have the men we know are the perfect match for us, and we will be married soon."

"In London?"

She sighed heavily. "I would much rather stay here. I believe I could quite happily live here, Colin, without wondering what the rest of the world was getting up to. We…we don't have to go south, do we?"

Colin brought his other arm around her and hugged her tightly. "If I could have my way, we'd spend fifty weeks of the year here and only spend a week in London and a week in Bath. But I suppose we might have to go and see your sister more often than that."

Olivia smiled. "And a few weeks to see my parents, of course."

Colin groaned. "Now, I have nothin' agen y'parents, lass…"

Olivia could not help but laugh. "Yes, they have been a bit much. But then they have had an awful shock! Isabella's news… I think it really was best for them to accompany us here."

"Then Harold owes me," said Colin darkly. "We could stay here for months, and no one would even care to disturb us. We could send your parents back to London."

It was a delightful thought. *Oh, to be alone*, thought Olivia. *Properly alone, in the castle. They would be able to…* "You have to marry me first!"

Colin sighed. "A few months and all the wedding plans will be ironed out."

Olivia smiled. *Was this the right opening?* "No, sooner."

He released her and stepped around to look into her face. He was frowning. "Why?"

This was an important moment, one she would never get again, and she had to make sure it was right. Besides, she could not keep it a secret much longer. Unlike Isabella, she was not one for secrets.

"Because," she said quietly, "I…I am with child. I do not believe we should leave it much longer before we wed!"

Olivia had expected him to be happy. She had thought he might kiss her or pull her into his arms. Sometimes she wondered whether he would cry.

But Colin did none of these things. Instead, he just stood there and laughed.

A twinge of panic rushed through Olivia's heart. Was he not excited?

"And what is so funny?" she said icily.

"Oh, Olivia, I mean no harm," Colin said hastily, still smiling. "'Tis just…I received this from Isabella and her husband this morning."

He pulled out a letter from his greatcoat pocket and handed it to her.

Olivia could not see the connection. "So?"

"So, they are expecting, too!" Colin said triumphantly.

Olivia laughed. "You–you are not serious! Maybe we aren't so different after all."

She was prevented from saying anything else by the fierce kiss that her future husband and the father of her child bestowed upon her.

EPILOGUE

COLIN GRINNED. "WHAT do you have to be nervous about?"

The man beside him smiled anxiously, though he had no right to be, as far as Colin was concerned. *Of the two of them, it was Colin who had the rather more difficult job.*

"Nervous?" said Jacob with a shake in his voice that echoed around the church. "I have never been anyone's best man before, and it is not as though I exactly have a great track record with weddings!"

Colin laughed but stopped abruptly. There was something about laughter in a church. It was not forbidden, not exactly, but it always felt a little wrong. A little rebellious. As though one had sworn before a vicar, something he had never done before but was liable to do today.

"Nonsense," he said, slapping the man on the shoulder. "Nothing to worry about."

Colin wished he could convince himself. He was about to wed the most beautiful, most charming, most perfect woman. She was the best choice he had ever made, the only choice he knew he would never regret.

Still…after having a wedding planned for the last two years, it felt a little strange to finally be standing at the front of the nave in a church, waiting for his bride to arrive. A different bride from who he had initially been expecting.

Olivia. She would be losing the name of Lymington and taking his own.

"Well, won't be long now," said Jacob bracingly. "Then I can return to being a husband and father, with none of this nonsense."

He grinned at Colin and then turned to look over his shoulder into the congregation that was starting to swell in number.

Colin's gaze followed his and saw Mrs. Beauvale and their two young children waving at them from the back of the church. And there was the Duke and Duchess of Axwick, kind of them to come.

Marnmouth had hardly been able to refuse their invitation, not after that rather bizarre altercation at the Larnwick ball, and there was Viscount Braedon and his new bride, who had given such terrible advice on that ride together.

And there was the Duke and Duchess of Mercia! Colin had nothing ill to say of the man, save that his formal dress was atrocious. But then, if the gossip were true, he'd barely spent a handful of years as real nobility.

His sister and her husband were behind them, and she was evidently trying to straighten her brother's cravat. Colin smiled at Viscount Donal, another outsider, an Irishman. He really must make sure they got together for a dinner or hand of cards while they were both in London. *There were few people he could abuse the English with.*

The Devonshires were here, which was something of an honor, Colin had been given to understand by his future in-laws. Olivia had agreed, though Colin could see nothing special about them. Nothing the Lenskeyns' didn't have, though his wife was formidable.

They were all here, along with half of London, it seemed to Colin. So much for a quiet wedding, but then, the Lymingtons were very popular people.

Well. A lot of people knew *about* them. Colin had given them entire *carte blanche* on the guest list, and because of that, one could find the best and brightest of society.

Each of them had their own incredible love stories, he was sure, though he only knew some of them in great detail. One day, he would have to encourage them to tell the full stories.

Just as he opened his mouth to ask Jacob what the scandal behind the Earl of Chester's marriage was, the entire church went silent, and the congregation rose to their feet.

Colin swallowed. His bride was here. There was no going back, thank God, for he had been sorely tempted to take his future bride into his arms during those long nights at Larnwick Castle and show her just what she was missing.

His jaw dropped. The doors at the end of the church had opened, and there in the doorway stood a vision of beauty and elegance. The gown was expertly tailored to fall like the waterfall they had espied on Cragon Hill, and as Miss Olivia Lymington stepped forward on her father's arm, Colin's heart skipped a beat.

The nerves vanished, melted away like a summer frost. He was where he should be, about to marry a woman that he loved.

By the time she reached the front of the nave, Colin smiled.

"You were still expecting me, weren't you?" she whispered.

Colin knew she was jesting, but there was still a hint of pain there.

He nodded and murmured, "I have been waiting for you for a long time, longer than I can say. I…I am so glad you are finally here."

They were the words that his future wife needed. As Mr. Lymington moved her hand to his and kissed his daughter's cheek, Colin knew this was a changing of the guard.

She was his now. His to love and protect.

The wedding service passed with a blur. It was impossible to tell what happened, for Colin was in a happy stupor. The only moment he recalled, and would of course never reveal to his wife, was when the vicar came to speak their names in the vows.

The rings were exchanged, and before he knew it, the vicar was beaming at them.

"I do pronounce you husband and wife!"

It was all Colin could do to resist kissing his beautiful bride. There was an audible sigh of contentment from the congregation, and though Colin sat through the rest of the church service in a daze, it was with his wife's hand in his.

Beside him sat not just Olivia, but his wife, Olivia Vaughn, Duchess of Larnwick. They had finally married and would spend the rest of their lives together with their children.

Colin's stomach lurched as they rose for the procession out of the church. *Children.* She was already pregnant with his child!

Being a parent was something he had always assumed would happen. He was a duke, and there needed to be another duke after him. That would require a certain about of legwork. But whether it was a boy to carry on the family name or a girl to honor it, he could not wait. His family with Olivia was only just beginning.

"And what is on that mind of yours?"

Colin jumped as they started walking toward the church door. Olivia was looking at him with that rather knowing look on her face which always disconcerted him.

But she did not have long to wait for an answer. As they stepped over the church threshold, Colin gave in to the desire he had been fighting ever since she had entered the church and pulled Olivia into his arms for a passionate kiss.

Isabella and her husband were waiting to greet them.

Colin glanced quickly at Olivia. It was their first official meeting in public, and there was no telling how much peace the two sisters had managed in that brief visit in Bath.

But he should not have doubted her. Olivia looked perfectly calm, even happy to see her sister.

Over her shoulder, Colin could see Mr. and Mrs. Lymington watching the four of them carefully.

"Isabella," said Olivia, holding out her hands.

And then they were embracing, tears in their eyes, as Colin looked on with amazement.

"Women," said Harold gruffly, holding out a hand. "Cannot pretend to understand them."

Colin did not hesitate. He accepted the handshake immediately, knowing a lifetime of good humor with one's brother-in-law was at stake if he faltered.

Damn, what a mess.

"I should have told you all I was already married!" Isabella was saying with a wry smile.

"And you can't blame me," said Harold with a laugh. "After a year, I thought you had been told and were just ignoring me!"

"Goodness, it sounds like misunderstandings all round," said Colin with a grin.

It might have been Colin's imagination, but Harold looked relieved at his words, and Colin felt a definite chill in the air disappear.

This was it, then—the beginning of something new and wonderful for the sisters.

"Goodness me," said Philip Egerton, the Earl of Marnmouth who was nearby. "And I thought the way we got married was wild! You know, no one expected that…no, Penelope FitzMarnmouth, put that boy down!"

Colin gaped as he watched the earl run off after a teenage girl who had been speaking to a footman. Penelope FitzMarnmouth? He was not aware the earl had any children?

"Ah, it feels a lifetime ago that we were married, don't you think, Richard?" said Tabitha St. Maur, the Duchess of Axwick.

Her husband shrugged. "It feels like just how long it was."

Olivia smiled. "I never heard the story."

Tabitha sighed, a wistful smile on her face. "Well, it all started at a wedding rather like this one. I watched the soft morning light fall through the stained glass windows…"

About Emily E K Murdoch

If you love falling in love, then you've come to the right place.

I am a historian and writer and have a varied career to date: from examining medieval manuscripts to designing museum exhibitions, to working as a researcher for the BBC to working for the National Trust.

My books range from England 1050 to Texas 1848, and I can't wait for you to fall in love with my heroes and heroines!

Follow me on twitter and instagram @emilyekmurdoch, find me on facebook at facebook.com/theemilyekmurdoch, and read my blog at www.emilyekmurdoch.com.

Made in the USA
Columbia, SC
17 April 2021

The
**Faith in
Action**
Series

Series Editor: Catherine Bowness

God of Surprises

The Story of Desmond Tutu

Andrew Ahmed and Vanessa Gray

Illustrated by Brian Platt

RELIGIOUS AND MORAL EDUCATION PRESS

GOD OF SURPRISES

The Story of Desmond Tutu

An eight-year-old boy was sitting in the playground at his new school watching the other children running around at lunchtime. He tried not to show how shocked he was to see them rummaging through the dustbins like tramps looking for scraps.

The boy, who was black, soon realized that these bins were filled not with scraps but with totally untouched school lunches discarded by pupils from the surrounding white-only schools. The white children got free lunches at school (even though most could afford to pay for them), but they preferred to eat packed lunches brought from home. The black and coloured children at the boy's school did not get free school food. The government said they could not afford to feed all the black children so they would not feed a single one of them. So the poorer black pupils learned from that early age that their needs were less important than those of the white children.

The country was South Africa in the late 1930s. The boy would grow up within the racist system of apartheid and live to see it collapse – he would become Archbishop Desmond Tutu.

Desmond Tutu was born on 7 October 1931. He went to a school that had only black and coloured pupils, because non-white people were not allowed in white schools in South Africa.

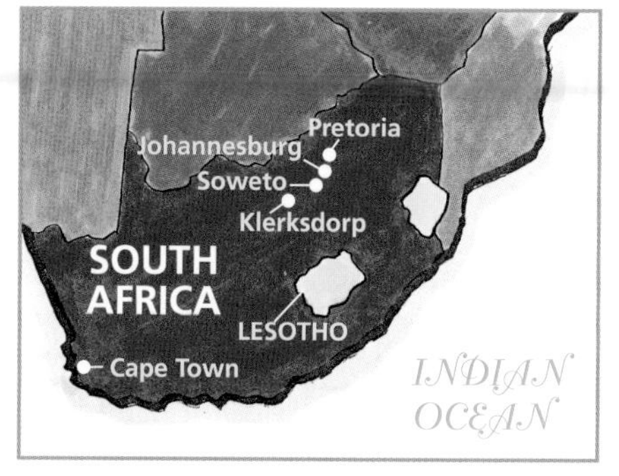

The all-white government divided races in South Africa into whites, coloureds (mixed race), Asians and blacks; but all non-whites were treated as 'black' on the whole. (Similarly, this book uses 'black' as a term for all non-whites who were treated as second-class citizens during apartheid rule.)

There was no clear way of identifying who would be labelled black, coloured or white. At one time the test was even as silly as putting a pencil in your hair: if it stayed there in your curls then you must be black, but if it dropped down a bit you were coloured and if it did not stay in at all then you must be white.

Black South Africans were seen by most of the white South Africans as fit for only the worst-paid, dirtiest work and had to keep a low profile in their own country.

All non-whites had to carry passbooks proving who they were and that they had a right to be where they were. They had to show their passbooks when stopped and were often searched by white police officers as if they were criminals. It was hard for black children to grow up seeing their parents and other role models humiliated in this way. Between 1916 and 1981, around a quarter of a million people were arrested for breaking the pass laws. On the whole though, non-white people accepted their unfair position in society: that was the way things were and they just had to make the best of it.

The Tutu family home was always warm, welcoming and better than many other black people's homes, but they still had no electricity or plumbed toilets. The house was really just a few rooms on a dirt road. Desmond had shorts and a shirt to wear to school, but no shoes. The school he went to at fourteen was impoverished as it was a 'blacks-only' school, but it had high standards and produced many future black leaders.

Desmond was not always saintly. He and his friend Stanley used to spend their monthly pocket money on 'roll-up' cigarettes, and his left-handedness caused lots of fights for space at the desk he shared with two other pupils. He had a wicked sense of humour, but was kind and gentle too. He was hopeless at maths but in most subjects he was unusually intelligent.

What Do You Think?

Important: in answering 'What Do You Think?' questions in this book, it is important that you not only state your opinion but also give as many reasons as possible for your opinion.

1. How far do you think the state of a school's buildings, the amount of money available to a school and the size of classes affects the pupils' education?

2. Children are often taught to respect their parents. Parents have the responsibility of showing children how to behave. When black children saw the police treating their parents like criminals, why might they have been (a) confused and (b) upset?

A Friend for Life

When he was fourteen, Desmond caught the disease tuberculosis (TB) and was kept in hospital for nearly two years. While he was in hospital he was visited every week by an English priest called Father Trevor Huddleston. Desmond had been staying at a hostel in Sophiatown because he could not afford the fare to get home from school at nights. The hostel was run by the Fathers of the Community of the Resurrection, a group of Christian priests to which Trevor Huddleston belonged.

Trevor Huddleston had worked in Sophiatown for thirteen years. He tried hard to make life better for the black people forced to live in this slum area. Here there was such extreme poverty that children were often homeless and sometimes starved to death. Huddleston believed that apartheid was clearly unchristian and evil and worked on projects such as opening a nursery school at night so that young homeless children could stay there to protect them from cold and sickness. He was also never afraid to challenge the police when they bullied and imprisoned black people for stupid reasons.

Desmond's long stay in hospital was the start of a life-long friendship with Trevor Huddleston. Desmond knew Huddleston was special when he raised his hat to Desmond's mother as a sign of respect, something he'd never dreamed of seeing a white man do to a black woman. Desmond has always marvelled at the relationship that developed between him and Trevor Huddleston: 'Who was I – just another black boy – that he should visit me?'

Lying in bed in hospital gave Desmond a lot of time to be still and think. He became more thoughtful and reflective, and developed a strong commitment to Christianity and a spiritual approach to life. He read constantly to keep himself entertained and also tried to keep up with his school work. He had a photographic memory, which meant he could recite any line from any page of a textbook he had read. He learnt a lot through all the reading he did and this gave him a more international and mature view on how a society could be.

Desmond's life has been hugely influenced by the humility, gentleness and selflessness of spiritual people like Trevor Huddleston.

What Do You Think?

1. Why did Trevor Huddleston make such a big impression on Desmond?

2. Desmond had to lie in bed being still and quiet as a hospital patient. During this time he thought about the Christian religion. Why do you think some religious believers find quiet times (a) a helpful part or (b) an essential part of their religious lives?

3. Missing two years of school through illness can be disastrous for a child's education. How may his long stay in hospital have helped Desmond in later life?

Teacher to Priest

After he left school, Desmond decided to train as a teacher, like his father. Three years before, a major change had occurred in how South Africa was ruled. In 1948 the National Party came to power by promising apartheid, to the white voters.

There were two main types of white settler in South Africa: the Dutch and the British. The descendants of Dutch settlers used a language called Afrikaans. In Afrikaans, the word 'apartheid' means 'apartness': in practice, apartheid meant separating black people from white people to keep the whites as rulers.

Non-whites could be punished with prison or fines for not carrying their passbooks. Marriage and sexual contact between whites and non-whites was made illegal and labelled immoral.

An eighteen-year-old white person could vote, but a black working adult could not and would be insultingly called 'boy' or 'girl' by white people regardless of their age. Perhaps treating black men and women as if they were children or animals made it easier to justify the whole apartheid system of disrespect and cruelty.

Black people could never relax in the usual places: they could not go into a café to buy a drink on a hot day as non-whites were not allowed in cafés, they could not sit or enjoy themselves out of doors as beaches and parks open to white people were forbidden territory for non-whites. It was as if the very skin of the native people was an offensive sight to the white community.

Many black people still accepted their unpleasant position in society – some turned to the Christian belief that they would have a better time in heaven. But Desmond was starting to meet people who were angry and wanted to bring the country back into the power of black South Africans. These people wanted a government 'of the African, by the African, for the African'.

In 1955, Desmond married Leah and went to teach at the high school next to his father's primary school. Studying there was hard as there might be as many as sixty pupils in a class, some of them adults who had had to work to support their families in between years of study. Desmond's passion and enthusiasm made him a popular teacher – he could even inspire the pupils to study maths, which he had been weak at himself.

He also created a desire in his pupils to use every chance to boost their opportunities in life. In most black schools teachers and students preferred using English because Afrikaans was seen as the language of the oppressors and speaking tribal languages just made black people seem even more different from the whites. Desmond taught his pupils to go one better than that and master all the languages they could. Some pupils called him 'braboy', meaning lovable or charming boy.

The all-white government had now passed the Bantu Education Act, which allowed black youngsters to study only subjects that prepared them for jobs such as working on farms or other manual labour.

When apartheid was introduced it was officially supposed to mean separate but equal development, but speakers in parliament revealed its true nature when they said that black people needed to be kept in their place in their mud huts. They had to provide labour for the whites and to study was only to try and imitate the white man. Black children were put to work with picks and shovels when they should have been reading and writing. Teachers were arrested and fined if they broke the law.

White Christians were fiercely divided in their views on apartheid and how far they should accept the government's laws. The mainstream Christian Churches refused to ban black people from churches in white areas but some churches followed racist practices such as seating black worshippers at the back and not letting them take Communion until the whites had finished. Many Afrikaaners (white South Africans descended from Dutch settlers) belonged to the Dutch Reformed Church. This Church did keep the races separated during services, and taught that apartheid was God's will.

The Community of the Resurrection, to which Desmond's great friend Father Huddleston belonged, were truly devoted to prayer but were also always there giving people practical help. Desmond became involved with this work for the oppressed and the suffering, helping when there were problems in the school or the villages. It rooted his faith in a down-to-earth way so that his religious beliefs were always closely connected to his understanding of people and their lives.

The education system for black pupils was collapsing so Desmond made the distressing decision to leave teaching. His thoughts now turned to becoming a priest.

What Do You Think?

1. Why do you think the government banned 'mixed marriages'?

2. Why do you think the Christian Churches had such opposing views on apartheid?

3. Desmond later said, 'Religion is not a form of escapism. Our God does not permit us to dwell in a kind of spiritual ghetto, cut off from the real life out there.' What do you think he meant?

4. Desmond has said 'We have to try as the Church to help the people in their immediate need, but that is just the short term. I think the long-term strategy of the churches is to continue to be a conscience of the community, pointing out how horrendous this system is, and how inconsistent with the gospel of Jesus Christ it must be.' What do you think he meant?

The Sharpeville Massacre

The African National Congress (ANC), led from 1991 until 1999 by Nelson Mandela, is now a leading political party in South Africa which represents the interests of all South Africans regardless of their race. In the 1950s, the ANC was just a group of mainly black politicians and campaigners who wanted to undo some of the most unjust laws and organized peaceful protests to achieve this. The volunteers in the campaign deliberately broke apartheid laws in such a way that they would put enough strain on the prisons and law courts to break down the whole system.

In 1960, events took a tragic turn when thousands of people deliberately left their passes at home one day and turned themselves in at police stations. The police in a town called Sharpeville panicked and suddenly opened fire on a quiet crowd. In the massacre 180 people were wounded and 69 killed – many of them shot in the back as they tried to flee.

There were other minor shooting incidents of this type around the country that day. Later furious crowds went on the rampage burning symbols of their repression such as the flag of the white government. A national day of mourning was held with a strike by all workers. The ANC and the Pan African Congress, another political party striving for the rights of the black community, were banned by the government, and anyone believed to be helping them could be sent to prison for ten years.

This was the year when Desmond was ordained as a deacon, the first stage in becoming a priest. He was still not thinking or acting in a political way, just learning to be a good priest and father to his three children. He does admit to being amazed sometimes at how long it took him to become involved in the struggle against apartheid. His first home as a deacon was a garage, into which he had to cram his whole young family. The conditions were appalling and inhumane for young children, and also for Desmond as a former TB sufferer, but the Tutu family accepted it all. In 1961, aged thirty, Desmond was ordained as a priest. He was given his own parish church and a proper house in a new township. A township was an area of slum housing where black people were forced to live to keep them in an easily controllable situation away from the white people.

Desmond was very aware of the importance of giving a powerful sermon and also loved being warmly welcomed into parishioners' homes. It was rewarding work: a satisfying job with people who loved having him as their priest. He had now truly found his vocation in visiting the needy, the sick and the dying and caring generally for his parishioners.

What Do You Think?

1. Were ANC members right to break laws deliberately? Give reasons.

2. Why do you think laws were passed making it difficult for black people to protest, when it was the white police who were responsible for the killings?

Holiday from Apartheid

Next came the golden opportunity that was to play such a large role in changing Desmond's view of apartheid by showing him how life could be for a black person outside a racist system. He was offered the chance to go to London for three years to study for a second degree in theology. In 1962, his wife and the two older children came to Britain to join Desmond, who had already been there a few months and was desperately lonely. The youngest child stayed with Desmond's mother and followed in 1963. In England that year the couple had their fourth child.

Being in Britain was a revelation for the family: they could walk anywhere without having to check for signs to tell them if they were allowed to be there. They admit that they struggled to stop being afraid of being arrested at any moment and they worried when they saw mixed-race couples walking together. 'It's difficult to express the sense of exhilaration, of liberation, of being made to feel human,' Desmond said of that time.

The Tutus would go for walks in the middle of the night just to relish the pleasure of not being accosted by a policeman demanding their passes. White people had to join queues behind Desmond for the first time and policemen treated him with courtesy whenever he asked a question. These were all new experiences for a black man from South Africa during apartheid. He was fortunate not to encounter any of the racism that was and is common in parts of Britain; as a visiting foreigner and a member of a church community he was protected from it.

He asked for a less-wealthy parish but was instead sent to a really rich parish where his humour and devotion won over the initially shocked parishioners. The Surrey village gave much to the Tutu family and Desmond more than repaid them by spending all his time helping out in village life, sharing his Christian love and joy. He also made people more aware of the situation of black South Africans.

Worship is an utterly fulfilling part of Desmond's life and he was once seen dancing with sheer joy around a churchyard all alone after Christmas Midnight Mass. This is the kind of love that people cannot help responding to despite themselves and it greatly enriches Christianity. Westerners often find it hard

to celebrate the love of God in an abandoned way that is filled with the joy of living. Desmond frees people to do just that in a simple yet beautiful manner.

After Desmond returned to South Africa, he found it very difficult being a second-class citizen again. He said it was lucky he was expected only to feel Christian love for a white man who demanded his passbook and not to like him. Desmond was lucky to get a job lecturing for the Community of the Resurrection at St Peter's, where he had far more freedom, equality and respect than he could have had in normal South African society.

Desmond felt it was important that black people were treated equally to whites: that they were not oppressed neither were they were given special favourable treatment. He set very high intellectual standards for himself and for his black students for this reason.

What Do You Think?

1. How did his experiences in England affect Desmond's attitude towards white people?

2. What do you think is the difference between Christian love and liking someone?

3. Is it possible to love a racist but hate racism? Give reasons.

A Turning-Point

Policing of the black community in the early 1960s was reaching horrific levels. People were disappearing into police custody and never being charged or released and there were terrible tales about the conditions in the prisons and torture by the security police. The ANC had been a peaceful protest party for fifty years. Now, under Nelson Mandela's leadership, it developed a paramilitary group (an unofficial army) whose role was to blow up or burn down factories and power stations, but not to kill or injure anyone. The aim was to make it so expensive to run South Africa under an apartheid system that the government would be forced to listen to the black South Africans. After a brief and fairly successful campaign, Mandela and other leaders were arrested and given life prison sentences.

Desmond had been in England during these events and missed this period of tension. He came back to the South African situation with fresh hope, energy and ideas for peaceful resistance at a time when a new approach was needed that had a more respectable and safe image than terrorism.

Groups started to develop to rebuild pride and strength in black people. Desmond was in general agreement with these radical groups, but they felt he was too moderate and optimistic about the future. He wanted black and white people to become friends and allies, whereas many of the black groups felt that black people had to withdraw and strengthen themselves before confronting whites as equals. Desmond did act politically sometimes, though, such as by refusing to meet VIPs he did not respect and making powerful public speeches criticizing apartheid.

His first dramatic act in the struggle for black rights came at a peaceful student protest that had suddenly been surrounded by armed police. Desmond forced his way in and broke up the tense stalemate, shepherding students away and making sure they got home safely whilst offering them encouragement and support. It was a turning-point for Desmond, who said he actually felt angry at God for allowing a situation where students could be trapped and terrorized by armed police. In church the next day he broke down in tears and from then on took part in the struggle in a new and more intense way. He became known to the authorities as a potential trouble-maker and also began to represent his Church in their response as Christians to apartheid.

What Do You Think?

1. What was the ANC trying to achieve through acts of sabotage at this time?

2. Was life imprisonment a fair sentence for Nelson Mandela? Give reasons.

3. Do you think that black people at this time were wiser to co-operate with the white government or should they have had as little to do with them as possible? Give reasons.

4. Desmond later said about a cartoon book called *My God*, 'My favourite shows God somewhat disconsolate and saying, "Oh dear, I think I have lost my copy of the divine plan." Looking at the state of the world you would be forgiven for wondering if He ever had one and whether He had not really botched things up.' Why might Desmond have felt that God carries some blame for the state of the world? What is your view on this idea?

Dean of Johannesburg

In 1970 his next job took him out of South Africa into bordering Lesotho. There he developed his thoughts on 'Black Theology' – how to apply the teachings of Christianity to the particular experiences of black people. As a Christian minister, his beliefs were based on the Bible, but his experiences as a black man in a racist society had also affected these beliefs. From his understanding of the Bible he saw that Christianity stresses that all people are equal and that God wants people to be free. Injustice and oppression go against God's wishes, so as a Christian he felt that he had a responsibility to help black people become equal in all senses with white people in South Africa. From his understanding of Jesus' teachings he also saw that Christians must bring about those changes without using violence.

Two years later Desmond took a job in England, then in 1975 he was offered the important post of Dean of Johannesburg. Should he accept? Leah clearly did not want to go back to South Africa, the younger children were enjoying school and had made friends in England, and their eldest child Trevor (named after Trevor Huddleston) had just begun a degree course in London. Also, if Desmond left his present job he would have to break his contract, which still had three years to run. He went on a retreat so that he could think clearly and seek God's advice in his thoughts and prayers. Eventually he decided he should go.

This post had always been held by white men so the deanery (dean's house) was in a white area. The Tutus refused this 'honour' and instead chose to live in Soweto – a sprawling black township of dreary and cheap slum housing. There was no electricity in Soweto, the roads were just dirt tracks and the air thick with pollution. Black people were delighted at the Tutus' decision, but there were some jealous complaints when the family decided to spend money on improving their house. Each day, in sharp contrast to their home, Desmond's work involved the running of the grand cathedral of Johannesburg.

The cathedral had a racially mixed congregation and clergy. Desmond brought in changes to the worship including shaking hands, hugging and kissing your neighbours on the cheek, which made many feel uncomfortable. His open-minded and loving approach did begin to win people over, though. He also supported the ordination of women as priests and revised sexist language whenever he came across it, which impressed many in his congregation.

What Do You Think?

1. Desmond has said, 'The Bible is the most revolutionary, the most radical book there is.' How does this compare with your impression of the Bible?

2. When offered the post of Dean, should Desmond have taken the views of his family into account more fully? Give reasons.

3. Is it preferable for an important leader or campaigner to be single or to be married with a family? Give reasons.

4. Why do you think the Tutus refused the offer of a big luxurious home?

A Loving and Lively Priest

One of Desmond's greatest strengths is the way he can blend in with any group, with Europeans he is European and with Africans he is African. He has been accused of not being African enough because he sent his children to boarding schools outside South Africa and spent so much time abroad in the company of non-South Africans. However, he has brought many gentle aspects of his African identity to the Church and the West, especially his slow dancing rhythm in worship, his celebration of African hymns and festivals, his lack of self-consciousness in bringing love and fun to traditional worship, and his knowledge of and pleasure in African languages, culture and people.

Desmond was always enthusiastic in his devotion to his friends and colleagues regardless of their feelings about it. Some were afraid to tell him of problems in their lives as they did not want the extra attention it would bring from him. An elderly man who made no secret of his dislike for Desmond was subjected to devoted regular visits from him whilst recovering in hospital from an operation.

Desmond's attention to detail is amazing and he will write to a post office commending a clerk on his good service or make sure he is there to greet someone coming out of prison with no-one else to meet them. The problem with this is that he expects as much attention in return and will sulk if a friend doesn't greet him enthusiastically enough or forgets an important date in his life.

Cruelty from the mass media, bitter critics and even those who have sent him death threats because of his work are something he, as an international figure, has had to learn to live with. The warmth of his Christian love tends to dominate the thoughts of most of those who have ever actually met him, though.

His daily life is filled with prayer and worship. He rises as early as 3.30 a.m. for an hour's prayer and celebrates Communion after breakfast. Short prayers are made between each of the day's activities, once a month he spends a day in retreat and each year he fasts, holds vigils and goes on longer retreats. Only the brave should be passengers in his car as they may be told to 'Shut up' so he can concentrate on his prayers (which he has been known to do with his eyes shut whilst driving along!).

The Soweto Massacre

In 1976 Desmond wrote to Prime Minister Vorster appealing to him on the shared humanity of all people, both black and white. He said that nothing could stop people from taking back their freedom and dignity, so white and black people needed to come together as fellow South Africans. He objected to the powers of the security police and courts and warned, 'I have a growing and nightmarish fear that unless something drastic is done very soon then bloodshed and violence are going to happen in South Africa almost inevitably.'

Soon after, 15 000 Soweto schoolchildren organized a peaceful march to protest at the single-race, low-standard education they were receiving and the use of the Afrikaans language by teachers. Armed police moved in and shot thirteen-year-old Hector Peterson dead – the first of six hundred schoolchildren, students and supporters to be killed over the next three weeks. When Desmond arrived he walked around talking to children and parents and crying with rage and sorrow in between. In church he said, 'We have been really shattered by the deafening silence from the white community ... What would you have done had they been white children? ... That is all we would have wanted you to have done.'

He also felt private pain since he knew he was about to leave his troubled people again to become Bishop of Lesotho. After the killings, he had decided to refuse the post, but the church authorities pressured him heavily. After weighing up all the conflicting advice and needs, he was devastated when he received official news that he had been chosen as bishop and must go. He had so much wanted to be a bishop, but not under such awful circumstances.

Desmond's return to South Africa came much sooner than he expected. In 1978 he joined the South African Council of Churches (SACC), which was beginning to come under increasing pressure from the government as their differences over apartheid grew. The SACC had declared that apartheid was against the teachings of Jesus so Desmond could speak out against apartheid in the name of Christianity and not as a politician. He also wanted to continue working in a parish and in 1980 his request was met. He became rector of St Augustine's in Soweto, a very poor parish even for Soweto, and he loved the challenge.

In 1978, few people realized that the new generation of black people were not going to submit to the barbaric system of apartheid as their parents had. Wealthier black people were starting to be able to get into a few public places such as international hotels, but the community as a whole were still kept as second-class citizens by apartheid. By now, 300 000 black people a year were being arrested for passbook offences and many black people were dying in custody. With so many organizations now banned, the SACC was one of the few groups that could be a voice for the silent black majority. Desmond wanted the SACC to act as a conscience for South Africans which would show how directly apartheid went against the teachings of Jesus.

One of the most offensive and brutal laws of apartheid was that black South Africans could be loaded into trucks by the government and taken to remote barren areas called 'Bantustans' or 'homelands'. Here they had to start their lives again without friends, family or familiar surroundings. More than 70% of the people in South Africa shared only 13% of the land. Some had to commute six hours per day to get to work while others were forced to leave their families and live in men-only hostels near their work. More than a few of those cast out into new and unknown areas literally starved. Desmond publicly declared that he was prepared to give his life to rid South Africa of the evil of apartheid's forced removals, which had begun in 1950.

The people in a village called Mogopa had been told they must move to another area as the Mogopa land would be more valuable to the whites. The villagers did not want to be thrown off their land, so when their houses were demolished they stayed put and rebuilt them. Desmond called on church leaders to come and join a vigil of protest, which they did. It did not stop the forced removal and the whites coming in and benefiting from that, but it did make a statement.

Desmond continued to campaign and speak out and spent a lot of time writing to people all over the world with requests relating to the South African situation. He warned all those who were not helping to end apartheid that once the liberation struggle had been won their refusals to help would not be forgotten. His speeches became more and more rousing and warned people that they would have to accept a very high price in lives lost to win the struggle, but that nothing could stop them as God was on their side:

> 'When God encounters injustice, oppression, exploitation, he takes sides ... Our God is not a God who sanctifies the status quo. He is a God of surprises, uprooting the powerful and the unjust to establish His Kingdom.'

In another speech, he dramatically promised to burn his Bible on the day that he was proved wrong about apartheid being an evil.

Desmond is a gentle man of peace and forgiveness, but he is also brave. Once, he stepped between security police and a black man they were beating. On another occasion he tried to save a black security policeman from an angry black crowd when they turned on him as a suspected informer, but unfortunately they killed the man later, after Desmond had gone.

What Do You Think?

1. Why do you think that a major biography of Desmond is entitled *Tutu: Voice of the Voiceless?*

2. Desmond is not always 'diplomatic' – his speeches can be quite harsh. His warning to people not helping to end apartheid seems to include a 'veiled threat'. Is it ever acceptable to use threatening language? Give reasons.

3. Desmond also said, 'My father used to say, "Don't raise your voice. Improve your argument." ' What is your view of this saying?

4. Is there any point in protesting against a situation which seems to be a 'lost cause'? Give reasons.

5. Was Desmond sensible to put himself at such risk? Give reasons.

The World Takes Notice

Desmond's studies and travels abroad brought him a growing audience for his views as a Christian on apartheid. He had a huge personal impact on those with whom he came into contact and this ensured they remembered what he had to say and listened sympathetically. He asked other countries to refuse to trade with or help South Africa unless the government ended apartheid.

In 1984, whilst visiting America, he was awarded the Nobel Peace Prize. He said it was really for all those who suffered under apartheid: for the devastated women trying to raise families alone, for their husbands forced to live in single-sex working hostels near the cities for eleven months of the year, for all those suffering daily indignities, in exile, banned, detained and even killed. When the Tutus returned to Johannesburg they were met by ecstatic crowds. The government was silent and media reports were brief, but since the award had been announced whilst Desmond was in America, the story received really good international media coverage. So the news spread far more quickly and widely than the South African government wished, and the whole world came to see Desmond as a symbol for the fight against apartheid.

Desmond with his wife and daughters at a press conference at London Airport in October 1984.

Soon after, Desmond became Bishop of Johannesburg, then in 1986 he was further promoted to Archbishop of Cape Town, the first black man to hold the position. He is affectionately known to many as 'Arch'.

There was great unrest in 1985. Black people were close to being at war with the police and hundreds were being killed. Tragically the black community was turning in on itself and executing suspected informers, a situation which the South African police exploited by spreading false rumours naming innocent black individuals as traitors.

Desmond spent much of his time conducting funerals of those killed. These also tended to become political demonstrations and he took great risks by angrily condemning the violence. In July 1985 he was at a township conducting the funeral of four young men who had died in an explosion. He urged a policy of peaceful protest, but as soon as the bodies were in the ground the crowds turned on a black man, accusing him of being a spy. They set fire to his car, saying that it would be his funeral pyre. While other bishops

present created a diversion, Desmond managed to drag the terrified and bleeding man into a safe car.

Ten days later a young mother was tortured to death at a funeral by a frenzied crowd who thought she was an informer. Desmond was so upset he said,

If you do that kind of thing again I will find it difficult to speak for the cause of liberation. If the violence continues, I will pack my bags, collect my family and leave this beautiful country that I love so passionately. I say to you that I condemn in the strongest possible terms what happened. Our cause is just and noble. That is why it will prevail and bring victory to us. You cannot use methods to attain the goal of liberation that our enemy will use against us.

The tension continued in 1986 with rioting and petrol bombings, and in less than two years, 1200 black people had been killed, mainly by the security forces. Then news came through of a large crowd assembled in the football stadium at the township of Alexandra. Desmond went to the stadium with other senior churchmen to try and calm the potentially dangerous situation but had to argue with armed soldiers for an hour before they let him through. He told the people that violent behaviour would weaken their cause and promised them God's help.

When the people had been moved to safety, he went to speak to the government on their behalf, but he had to take back the bad news that none of their requests for human rights were to be granted. The mob were frustrated and angry and booed him for having failed them. They swore to use their own methods from there on and not listen to him. This was a time when his support for non-violent methods was tested to the full as it put him in a position where he looked powerless. As time went on he did grow more and more sympathetic to the idea of a violent response to such a violent government.

What Do You Think?

1. In what ways did international publicity help the black people's cause in South Africa?

2. Explain in your own words what Desmond meant by 'You cannot use methods to attain the goal of liberation that our enemy will use against us.'

A New Era for South Africa

In 1986 President Reagan of the USA said that he did not support economic sanctions against South Africa (e.g. restricting trade). Desmond responded with rage and said it was 'nauseating' and America could 'go to hell'. This was typically outspoken behaviour for Desmond. He has always claimed he is just a churchman and not a politician, though he has never been afraid to speak against injustice: 'I am a church person who believes that religion does not just deal with a certain compartment of life. Religion has a relevance for the whole of life and we have to say whether a particular policy is consistent with the policy of Jesus Christ or not.'

That year the South African government finally announced an end to the pass laws. This gave black people more freedom, but to do what, since the overall situation remained the same? Desmond said it was 'too little too late'.

In 1989, he joined a protest against beach apartheid in South Africa. The media representatives were arrested for being there and protesters were warned that live ammunition and other forceful methods could be used to disperse them if necessary.

Huge changes at last began to come about after the election of F. W. De Klerk as President in 1989. Within a year the ban on the ANC and PAC was lifted and Nelson Mandela was released. This event was televised live around the world and symbolized freedom for all black South Africans after so many years of suffering. Mandela could have come out of prison full of bitterness and hatred, ready to punish the Afrikaaners, but he was forgiving and thoughtful – only looking ahead to build a good future.

This launched a long series of meetings where the government and the ANC tried to find a way forward to a form of power-sharing without it leading to huge bloodshed. Two major problems were the desire of the Zulu tribe to assert themselves in a powerful political position and also the vicious backlash from some Afrikaaners who feared losing their position in society. Many died in this turbulent but necessary period. Desmond was at full stretch helping to keep the political situation moving and the public mood as calm as possible.

In 1993 exclusive white rule finally ended. The result of the first democratic elections was that in 1994 Nelson Mandela became the first black South African President, heading an ANC government. By 1996 there was a new constitution aimed at creating full racial equality and harmony. Mandela said that black South Africans were imprisoned not only by apartheid laws, but also by homelessness, despair and the racism of the mind. He argued that quiet but firm steps had to be taken to undo the effects of the past.

What Do You Think?

1. In Britain, if it rains on General Election day some people do not go to the polling-station. In 1994, when democratic elections were held in South Africa, some members of the black community walked over 10 miles to reach a polling-station, whilst others queued all night so as not to miss their chance to vote. Why do you think attitudes and actions in the two countries are different? Should people be made to vote in democratic elections? Give reasons.

The Challenge of Reconciliation

Mandela saw forgiveness as the guiding force for his new government: 'I wanted South Africa to see that I loved even my enemies while I hated the system that turned us against one another.' The aim was to forgive but never to forget what happened under apartheid.

A process of sorting through the violent past of the apartheid era was also begun by the Truth and Reconciliation Commission, to ensure that all crimes were honestly acknowledged. Desmond Tutu played a key role in the commission, which threw light on many painful incidents. Those questioned were rewarded if they were honest and tried to clear up cases of people who had simply disappeared or whose deaths remained a mystery. The commission was not seeking revenge or to punish those who had enforced apartheid. It just tried to find out and document the truth about all crimes committed during apartheid – by both black and white.

The hardest challenge facing bereaved families was not only to forgive those who had caused their suffering, but to make sure that forgiveness was complete and unconditional – as with Christian love. This would mean the new South Africa could grow from strong roots, unaffected by blame or bitterness.

Desmond answers a question at a press conference soon after his appointment to the Truth and Reconciliation Commission.

In 1979, Desmond had written in his book *Crying in the Wilderness*:

'Basically I long and work for a South Africa that is more open and more just; where people count and where they will have equal access to the good things of life, with equal opportunity to live, work and learn. I long for a South Africa where there will be equal and untrammelled access to the courts of the land, where detention without trial will be a thing of the hoary past, where bannings and such arbitrary acts will no longer be even so much as mentioned, and where the rule of law will hold sway in the fullest sense. In addition, all adults will participate fully in political decision making, and in other decisions which affect their lives. Consequently they will have the vote and be eligible for election to all public offices. This South Africa will have integrity of territory with a common citizenship, and all the rights and privileges that go with such a citizenship, belonging to all its inhabitants.'

The new South Africa has a long way to go to bring about prosperity and social equality for everyone, but the situation has already changed out of all recognition, thanks to the work of Desmond Tutu and others who struggled to end apartheid.

In 1991 he said,

'At home in South Africa I have sometimes said in big meetings where you have black and white together ... 'Look at your hands – different colours representing different people. You are the rainbow people of God.' And you remember the rainbow in the Bible is the sign of peace. The rainbow is the sign of prosperity. We want peace, prosperity and justice and we can have it when all the people of God, the rainbow people of God, work together.'

God bless Africa
Guard her children
Guide her rulers
And give her peace.

Prayer, Father Trevor Huddleston

Biographical Notes

1913	Natives Land Act puts most land into white ownership. Further segregation laws follow.
1931	Desmond Mpilo Tutu born in Klerksdorp, South Africa.
1948	National Party voted into government by white people.
1949	Prohibition of Mixed Marriages Act.
1950	All South Africans grouped according to race in a register. Group Areas Act enforces the divide of races in towns.
1951	Tutu goes to teacher-training college.
1953	Bantu Education Act changes education for black children.
1955	Tutu marries Nomalizo Leah Shenxane.
1958	Tutu leaves teaching to train as a priest.
1960	Sharpeville Massacre. ANC and PAC banned. Tutu ordained as a deacon.
1961	Tutu ordained as a priest.
1962	Tutu starts studying for a master's degree in theology at King's College, London. His family join him in England.
1964	Nelson Mandela and other ANC leaders jailed for life.
1967	Tutu returns to South Africa and teaches at St Peter's College (run by the Community of the Resurrection).
1970	Tutu moves to a teaching job in Lesotho.
1972	Tutu takes job in England.
1975	Tutu appointed Dean of Johannesburg.
1976	Soweto Massacre. Tutu elected Bishop of Lesotho.
1978	Tutu becomes General Secretary of SACC.
1980	New wave of protests, strikes and school boycotts in South Africa.
1984	Tutu awarded Nobel Peace Prize. Tutu appointed Bishop of Johannesburg.
1985	State of Emergency declared (a regular feature from now on). Economic pressure from other countries begins to have real effects on South Africa.
1986	Tutu declares support for sanctions. Tutu elected Archbishop of Cape Town. Pass laws scrapped.
1988	Tutu starts to travel widely, campaigning against apartheid.
1989	F. W. De Klerk becomes President of South Africa.
1990	Ban on ANC and PAC lifted. Nelson Mandela released.
1993	Exclusive white rule comes to an end.
1994	First democratic elections. Mandela becomes President.
1996	New constitution with full racial equality

Things to Do

1. Draw a large map of the countries of Southern Africa. Identify and mark the places referred to in this book with symbols associated with events that happened there.

2. Imagine you are a black schoolchild in South Africa in the 1950s. Write a diary account of a typical week in your life.

3. Produce a cartoon strip on a dramatic incident in Desmond Tutu's life.

4. Design a stylishly produced newspaper front page reporting one of the following:

   (a) The Sharpville Massacre
   (b) The release of Nelson Mandela from prison
   (c) The ending of apartheid laws

5. In groups, improvise a dramatic sketch based on the following incident, with different people taking turns to play Desmond Tutu:

   A policeman has just beaten a black youth unconscious. An angry but unarmed crowd gathers and two more armed policemen arrive. Just as the situation is in danger of turning very nasty, Desmond Tutu arrives. What does he say and do to defuse the situation?

6. Watch the video *Cry Freedom* then write a personal response to the story.

7. (a) Find out how other countries and individuals boycotted South Africa during the years of apartheid rule. Explain the purpose of the boycotts and what effect they had on the people (black and white) in South Africa.

   (b) Some companies are boycotted by many people today, often because of their poor record on human rights, animal rights or the environment. Do some research to find out about some of these campaigns and offer your views on them.

8 Pastor Niemoller, a famous churchman imprisoned by the Nazis during the Second World War, wrote from a concentration camp:

> First they came for the Jews,
> And I did not speak out because I was not a Jew.
> Then they came for the communists,
> And I did not speak out because I was not a communist.
> Then they came for the trades unionists,
> And I did not speak out because I was not a trades unionist.
> Then they came for me,
> And there was no one left to speak out for me.

(a) Show how this verse might be applied to the years of apartheid rule in South Africa, and explain what Niemoller was trying to warn us about.

(b) Adapt the verse to apply to injustice in your society.

9 Design a poster which could be used by the Truth and Reconciliation Commission.

10 The Truth and Reconciliation Commission's policy is 'To forgive and not forget'. A typical case would be where a white policeman has confessed to killing a black child by shooting him/her in the back twenty years ago. Try to use the skill of empathy to write the following three letters:

(a) To the commission from the policeman, who admits the deed and is seeking an amnesty.

(b) To the commission from the parents, who have been informed of the facts and want justice.

(c) To the parents from Desmond Tutu, explaining the commission's decision to grant the policeman an amnesty.

11 Find out about another country in which a group or groups of people are suffering injustice. Produce a collage illustrating both their problems and a way forward.

12 Imagine that Desmond Tutu is coming to visit your town or community and will speak at a local church. He has asked you to help him write his speech. What will you suggest he includes?

13 Many of the world's top rock and pop artists played at a special 70th birthday concert for Nelson Mandela. Imagine a big concert is being held in honour of Desmond Tutu. Write a song lyric for your favourite artist or group to perform at the gig.

Questions for Assessment or Examination Candidates

14 Answer **one** of the following structured questions:

(a) Explain how Christians might use biblical teachings in a discussion about racism. (8 marks)

(b) Describe how and explain why Desmond Tutu has been working to achieve justice for people in South Africa. (7 marks)

(c) 'If you want justice you have to fight for it.' Do you agree? Give reasons to support your answer and show that you have thought about different points of view. You must refer to religious beliefs in your answer. (5 marks)

OR

(a) Describe and explain how Christian beliefs have influenced Desmond Tutu's fight against apartheid in South Africa. (8 marks)

(b) Describe and explain the different responses made by the Churches in South Africa to apartheid. (7 marks)

(c) 'Christians should not be involved in politics.' Do you agree? Give reasons to support your answer and show that you have thought about different points of view. (5 marks)

Religious and Moral Education Press
A division of SCM–Canterbury Press Ltd,
a wholly owned subsidiary of
Hymns Ancient & Modern Ltd
St Mary's Works, St Mary's Plain
Norwich, Norfolk NR3 3BH

First published 1999

ISBN 1 85175 173 4

Designed and typeset by
TOPICS – The Creative Partnership,
Exeter

Printed in Great Britain by
Brightsea Press, Exeter for
SCM–Canterbury Press Ltd, Norwich

Notes for Teachers

The first Faith in Action books were published in the late 1970s and the series has remained popular with both teachers and pupils. However, much in education has changed over the last twenty years, such as the development of both new examination syllabuses in Religious Studies and local agreed syllabuses for Religious Education which place more emphasis on pupils' own understanding, interpretation and evaluation of religious belief and practice, rather than a simple knowledge of events. This has encouraged us to amend the style of the Faith in Action Series to make it more suitable for today's classroom.

The aim is, as before, to tell the stories of people who have lived and acted according to their faith, but we have included alongside the main story questions which will encourage pupils to think about the reasons for the behaviour of our main characters and to empathize with the situations in which they found themselves. We hope that pupils will also be able to relate some of the issues in the stories to other issues in modern society, either in their own area or on a global scale.

The 'What Do You Think?' questions may be used for group or class discussion or for short written exercises. The 'Things to Do' at the end of the story include ideas for longer activities and more-structured questions suitable for assessment or examination practice.

In line with current syllabus requirements, as Britain is now a multifaith society, Faith in Action characters will be selected from a wide variety of faith backgrounds and many of the questions may be answered from the perspective of more than one faith.

CMB, 1997

Acknowledgements
Photographs are reproduced by kind permission of Popperfoto/Reuter (cover, page 18) and Popperfoto/UPI (pages 15, 16).